CrossTIME Science Fiction Anthology

featuring the winners of the
2002 Paul B. Duquette Memorial
Short Science Fiction Contest

CrossTIME
an imprint of the Crossquarter Publishing Group
PO Box 8756
Santa Fe, NM 87504-8756

CrossTIME Science Fiction Anthology
Copyright © 2002 Crossquarter Publishing Group
some images © 2003 www.clipart.com

ISBN: 1-890109-05-3 All rights reserved.

Printed in the United States of America on recycled paper.

The 2002 Winners

CrossTIME is happy to introduce the winners of the 2002 Paul B. Duquette Memorial Short Science Fiction Contest.

First place – "A Jolt to the System"
        by Margaret Yang and Harry R. Campion
Second place – "A Friend in Need…"
        by Richard O. C. Cousens
Third place – "Finding Magic" by F. I. Goldhaber
Fourth place – "The Sunspot" by Diane Masiello

Honorable mentions to:
"Cetacea" by L. J. Anderson
"Academic Freedom" by Richard Ferris
"Young at Heart" by John Hope
"The Hunt" by Jaylyn Jensen
"World Without End" by Kenra J. Miller
"A Rhesus to Believe" by Greg Stoker
"The Waiting Game" and "The Builder" by Ellen Straw

For simplicity, the stories are presented in alphabetical order by the authors' last names.

Therese Francis, publisher

In Memory
Paul B. Duquette (1953-2001)

Cetacea

L. J. Anderson

Somewhere off the south shore of StarRise Island, a dolphin was singing...

Cetacea, Odontoceti, Delphinidae, Tursiops Truncatus... Flipper. It was an ancient song from long long ago. It contained the order of their kind; family, genus and the names of the ones that had traveled upon the starships of man to this New World that was now their home. Her name was also in it, but it was not one of the first hundred. Her name was older still. Dolphins five thousand years dead had sung the song on Terra. Its haunting sounds and mournful cries echoing through the oceans of a dying world so far away that its star could not be seen.

The pod leader broke the surface, snatched a fresh breath and the song went on. The dolphin's name was Bridget. Her name honored one of their kind that had swam the sterile tanks of a lost place, the Sea World. Whatever a sea world was Bridget did not know or truly care. But she was proud of her name and sang it extra loud when she came to it. Most of the names were unknown to those that walked the land, but her kind remembered them all... Dolphins, Sea People, Fins, those who live below... Fishface.

The last had drawn quick responses from the two young bulls swimming with her and a big raspberry from her daughter. They told Bridget in crude and graphic detail what hole to shove her addition to the song into. One offered to help and she barrel-rolled while blowing bubbles, laughing...

The big cow was ten feet long and in the prime of her life, but her body bore the marks of hard living. A stranding two years past had discolored her gray back. Her skin was marred by scars and nicks from food that had not wanted to be eaten, along with love bites from amorous bulls she had paired with over the years.

The sea could be a cruel, unforgiving place and Bridget had taken a full measure of it. Bridget was a wild dolphin; a true free spirit of the sea that had little or no contact with man until one had found her stranded and near death, touched her heart, took her soul and changed her forever.

Bridget's name was known across the breadth of the Eastern Ocean. This hard-swimming female had crossed the great current of the Eastern Sea with its whirlpools and eddies, then turned and re-crossed it on a dare from a young bull that did not survive his own challenge.

Bridget still remembered the look on the face of the sleepy young boy when she had swam in at the head of her small pod and boldly entered the dolphin pool within the base of the cliff upon which the great keep stood.

The massive pile of stone had served as the headquarters for the dolphins and the humans that were their partners from before the first landing. Who had built it was never known and no other trace of them had been found.

She had rung the summoning bell smartly in report sequence and the boy had run shouting for his master that strange fins were in the pool.

The master was equally surprised when she had given her name and volunteered their service to those who walked the land. For he too had heard of this femme fatale that swam the deep ocean where most Tursiops did not normally fair.

But Bridget was of the *offshore* ecotype. Her form was well suited for deep diving, the larger body helping to conserve the body's heat. But all of dolphinkind had that sleek, streamlined, fusiform body shape and forever grin that had endeared them to mankind long before the two species had learned to talk to each other.

Bridget paused in her song as she was snapped back to reality by the click whistle speech of her kind. She knew who was speaking just by the feel of her voice in the water, it was Ruby. She was searching farther offshore where the water changed from blue-green to the dark blue of the deep ocean. "What have you found, Ruby?"

"Tuna… large school." Her reply sang through the water.

That would be welcome news, she thought to herself. "Good find, swim quickly until you can hear Leara and relay the information back to the fish master. He will send a boat to collect them, I recommend that he take a ten-member pod with him. If the school is as large as you say, he will need the extra bodies to control them and Ruby… no stopping for play, deliver message and return."

"Understood," Ruby's short reply drifted back to the threesome.

Bridget made a mental note to herself. She was going to chew Leara's tail off when she returned. The older dolphin had drifted off station breaking the communication chain that ran between the islands that made up the eastern ring that surrounded the caldera of the long dead super volcano. Bridget understood that relay duty was one of the most boring duties a fin could be assigned. It consisted of days orbiting on station, waiting and listening for any message that might be whispered into the sea. But it was important nonetheless; the radios that had been brought from old earth so long ago would, for some reason, not work on this New World.

She would speak to Commander Trencamp about shortening the on station time and increasing the rotation rate. The triad swam on…

Bridget was a senior fin; fish patrol was not one of her normal duties. But she had needed desperately to get away from the keep.

Dolphins could understand human speech and hear the thoughts of some. As man had found in his own kind, so it was with dolphins also. Some could hear thoughts better than others. Bridget could hear humans quite clearly and the broadcastings of the men and women within the keep were getting to her.

She understood this was to be her lot for the rest of her life and she would have to come to grips with her sensitivity. But for all her ability she could not feel the one man whose thoughts she so desperately wanted to hear more than all others.

The man Bridget had chosen could never truly be a dolphin

friend because his disability would always stand between them, but she did not care. To Bridget, Andy was "her" partner and that was the end of the matter. What others might think of this strange pairing mattered not at all to the pod leader. She would work with whoever was assigned to her, would even be friends with some of them, but the handsome young man who could not hear her thoughts had her heart and her soul.

The last straw had been when an argument had broken out between two of the humans. A female human had struck one of the young males. Bridget had been amazed that he had not struck the female back. If any dolphin had done such a thing they would have felt her tail flukes so hard they would not have been able to swim straight.

She had needed desperately to get away and seized the first opportunity that presented itself. Bridget had bumped the younger dolphin that had been assigned to lead this patrol and set a quick pace away from the keep.

⟨フ⟩

The night before, aboard the inter-island barge *Talofa*, south of StarRise Island…

The captain stood at the wheel, straining against the fury of the storm. He had sent his children below decks as the full might of the storm had struck and thereby sealed their fate.

The wild weather had blown up out of nowhere, catching him by surprise. The great waves crashed into then rolled over the *Talofa*. The old barge struggled to raise her bow above the crest of the following wave, but to no avail.

The swell rolled over the deck smashing into and snapping the mainmast. The wreckage vanished over the side, washed away by the following swell. The barge was now at the mercy of the storm that was pushing it ever closer to the reef.

The roar of the waves as they spent their fury against the coral ridge could be heard clearly by the men aboard the stricken barge. The captain gave his crew that was desperately trying to rig a makeshift sea anchor, leave to abandon ship if they so chose or to ride her in.

Quitting the now useless helm, he struggled across the heaving deck to the companionway leading below. Releasing the dogs of the hatch, he pulled it open and staggered across the forward hold. He regretted his greed that had blinded him to the danger of such a passage. But the sum offered by the stranger to take a shipment to StarRise Island and ask no questions had been too much to resist. Now he, the crew and his family would pay the price.

The captain was halfway across the hold when the *Talofa* was lifted up by the sea and smashed onto the reef. He was thrown violently against the starboard side and lay stunned by the impact, only to be washed across the hold to the portside by the force of the in-rushing water. But the raging storm was not done with the barge yet. It lifted her up once more and smashed the *Talofa* back down upon the reef.

What had been a flood became a wall of water; it filled the now pitch black hold in a heartbeat. The wave's backwash pulled the mortally wounded barge free of the coral and the following one forced her under. She flipped over as she sank downward. The wreck came to rest at last, upside down upon the sand-covered ledge at the base of the seaward side of the reef.

The captain was disoriented in the black water-filled void that would be his grave. He fought against the rising fear in his mind and tried to think his way out. He stopped struggling and the air within his lungs caused his body to rise. He now knew which way was up... and encountered the bottom of the overturned hull.

Diving down he searched for the hatch through which he had entered and found his way blocked by the sandy bottom. The need to breathe was becoming overpowering, kicking away from the deck he clawed frantically at the hull bottom above, tearing the very nails from his fingers in a vain attempt to gain his freedom as panic overcame him at last.

His end was upon him, the body's desire to breathe could be denied for only so long. The final exhalation of his life came out as a bubbling scream of terror and desperation that was swallowed up by the black water around him. He drew in a deep draft of the liquid that was to kill him and the doomed sailor went into spasms, his body attempted the impossible as it tried to clear the fluid from his lungs.

The convulsive movements soon lessened then ceased altogether. The now lifeless body floated in the darkness, a victim of an unforgiving sea that had no tolerance for fools and their stupidity or their avarice…

⟨⟩

On the seaward side of the reef the day after the storm, south coast of StarRise Island…. The bottom topography was changing. Instead of a gently sloping plain, the mountain that was StarRise Island made three stair steps into the ocean, then fell into the black abyss where no dolphin could go.

⟨⟩

The trio soared above the reef that had grown over eons upon the uppermost terrace, building ever closer to the edge, but held at bay by the power of the wide ocean beyond.

"Bridget, did you hear that?" The bull next to her spoke using the ultrasonic click- whistle speech that was the language of the Sea People.

Bridget glanced at the dolphin that swam close to her. "Hear what, Marco?" she asked.

He was silent for a moment as he swam beside her, "I don't know, just something. Sounds like it's coming from the leeward side of the reef. Can I look into it, pod leader?" the young bull asked.

"Very well, but stay within hailing distance," Bridget replied.

"Will do, Bridget!" He broke away from the group sweeping over the peak of the reef to disappear from sight.

Jasmine swam close to her dam's side. "Mother, isn't he just the most handsome bull you have ever seen!"

Bridget cast an appraising eye over her daughter and realized the she was no longer a little calf. Instead Bridget saw a well-formed female fin, with fine sleek bodylines and a big wide tail that was sure to drive all the boys wild.

Bridget sighed and the bubbles rose sparkling like silver jewels towards the surface. "Does he bite?" she asked quietly.

"Oh no! I mean, he is… very well-mannered." If dolphins could blush, Jasmine would have been red from beak to tail as she realized what her words revealed to her mother.

"That's good." Bridget smiled inwardly, remembering her own youth… first heat was always the hottest.

Mother and daughter porpoised together, then dove once more. "Jas, I could swear I heard Marco calling… maybe you should go see what he wants." Jasmine glanced at her mother for a moment not understanding

"I didn't hear... oh! Mom you're the coolest!" Jasmine shot away in powerful tail strokes.

Enjoy yourself, imp, Bridget thought to herself as she watched her daughter disappear into the blue-green haze of distortion and distance. Bridget continued moving eastwards along the reef's edge, alone in a noisy sea. The pod leader had not swum far, when she crossed over the outer perimeter of the debris field. Hmmm, the things lying upon the bottom had been made by the hands of man; they did not belong in the water.

A few moments later Bridget spotted the capsized barge lying on the sand-covered ledge twenty feet below the sun-dappled surface above. Bridget watched, as the unstable sand slipped over the edge of the precipice to fall in a cloud to the bottom far below.

She ghosted closer to the wreck... what idiot of a captain would bring this scow out to try his luck upon the sea? The old barge had been shoddily built and age had done her no favors. She should have been decommissioned long ago, but the dolphin had learned that humans could be so very stupid sometimes.

Bridget traversed the port side; gliding silently through the clear water. A quick look was all that was needed. Bridget could tell it had not been down long, since last night at the most. Even as she watched, a forlorn bubble of air slipped free from the dead hulk, its shape oscillating and shifting as it rose towards the surface.

Crossing over the bow, she traversed the starboard side to the site of the deathblow; what was that? Her thoughts raced as she back flipped, retracing her path listening for the sound to be repeated; back and forth she swam, but heard nothing. So Bridget moved off towards the hole that had been ripped in the barge's flank.

Poking her head inside with her sonar clicking, Bridget read the returning echoes that painted a macabre scene within the fin's mind. The interior was chaos, a jumble of loose cargo and rope lying about like sea snakes waiting to snare the unwary. A man's body floated, arms dangling, trapped by the hull bottom above. The corpse's mouth was agape; its sightless empty eyes stared forever at nothing.

Bridget entered the wreck, moving with caution so as not to disturb the debris scattered within. With her sonar going almost nonstop, Bridget scanned for anything that might be salvageable.

Feeling the need to breathe, the fin turned to leave when her sonar returns showed a large air pocket trapped in one corner. Why swim out when what she wanted was right there? Breaking the water's surface, she exhaled loudly and her ears were assaulted by white noise in the stygian blackness!

In a heartbeat she was underwater and racing away before her mind recognized the noise for what it was... the screaming of a terrified human. Bridget fought to slow her racing heart and the shakes running through her body. Steeling herself, she poked her head back into the air bubble and the screaming began a new.

"Please stop, I won't hurt you," the fin spoke into the darkness.

The scream stopped as if cut off by a knife. "Who... who's there?" A small timid voice asked.

"Bridget here. Help you I will." The shock of finding life where she had expected only death had affected Bridget and she was not speaking as well as she could.

"Cory! Someone's here to help us!"

Another small voice answered, "No! It's a monster, come to take us down into the black below!" Bridget could hardly believe it. Not one, but two had somehow survived, trapped in the terrible darkness knowing they were doomed to die.

Bridget not monster, Bridget is dolphin! She sent her thoughts into the terrified minds she felt in the blackness.

"I told you so." The first voice said.

Cory, I come to you. Touch me and see I am no monster, Bridget spoke softly within their minds.

They were young, Bridget surmised by listening to their voices. One male, one female and they both had the gift. The last part of the conversation had taken place within their minds. There had been no words spoken, but they were unaware of this because of the total darkness that surrounded them.

The fin swam towards the second disembodied voice. The dolphin was as blind in the blackness as were the children. With her rostrum above water the dolphin's sonar was useless.

Bridget was a mother with grown children of her own and it showed in the timber of her mind's voice. *Cory... I'm here. Reach out, touch me little one and know that I am not of the dark.*

A hand splashed the water looking for her and Bridget swam to the noise. Small fingers jerked away from the contact only to return hesitantly to touch her forehead and slide down the beak of her mouth to touch the peg shaped teeth it contained.

"She's real, Jyn!" He cried out into the darkness.

"Of course she is silly, this time it's not a dream!"

Bridget spoke, "Children, I must leave you...," and was interrupted by a choirs of pleading entreaties begging her not to go. "Enough!" It came out with more force than intended. "I will not be gone long, there are other dolphins close by, we will come back quick and get you out."

The first voice, that of the older female said "Please hurry Bridget, it's so scary here in the dark alone!"

Bridget put all the love and tenderness she could into her reply. "Little ones you have been so very, very brave! Be brave for just a little while longer and we will get you back to the world above. This bad dream will be over!"

The splash of her tail slapping the water echoed within the confined space as the dolphin submerged and left them alone in the darkness once more...

Bridget moved with as much dispatch as possible. Slipping through the breach in the hull, she looped up and over the wreck trailing a shimmering track of bubbles as she crossed the top of the reef. Bridget shouted for Marco and Jasmine at the top her voice.

☽☾

The leeward side of the reef, same time... Jasmine slipped quietly through the water following his sonar clicks as Marco diligently carried out a search pattern noting anything of interest to report to Bridget. Jasmine approached from above and behind him with a clear view of Marco swimming below as she began to sing softly in primal delphin, crafting a song of her willingness and her desire...

The fantasy began deep within his mind, he was unaware of it at first, but as it began to spread outward he slipped fully into his daydream. It was an erotic dream of female fins that flashed their firm white underbellies at him provocatively...

"Hello Marco." The sultry sonic voice filled the water around him, shattering the dream into a thousand tiny shards. But one did not disappear. In fact she was close and getting closer. "Marco, we've got to stop meeting like this," she dropped her jaw in a dolphin grin.

Jasmine rolled, showing off a beautiful white underbelly like those he had moments ago been dreaming of. As the last few inches of free water between them vanished, Marco's dark eyes took on a dreamy faraway look as their bodies touched for the first time. The world evanesced about them until only they two existed, one for the other held close within the warm bosom of the sea.

"Marco, Jasmine... Report! Hey you two talk to me; this is not a drill!"

Jasmine cried out in frustration as she fell away from her paramour and they smashed back into realty. "I... am going to bite my mother! I am really going to do it this time!!!" All the while Bridget was still shouting away with her sonar as she came into view. "Ok, mother! Tone it down will ya?"

Bridget clicked out a terse reply, "Up! Breathe, swim hard, will explain as we go." The triune swam at speed back the way Bridget had come.

"Marco I found your funny noise, a shipwreck with survivors trapped inside." The two young dolphins swam close.

"What?" Marco replied in amazement.

"Yes, two children trapped in an air pocket just forward of amidships," Bridget said with sharp staccato pops of her sonar.

Her daughter was the first to speak when they topped the reef and the wreck site came into view. "I don't like the looks of this... it does not look very stable, it could go over the edge at any moment."

The trio moved in silence for a space, "Look at the sand slide, not good, not good at all!" Marco added from Bridget's left side.

"At least it's not very deep, we won't have to worry about

bends sickness," Bridget clicked out to the pair swimming with her.

"That's true," Jasmine answered her mother. "And little children are not going to be able to hold their breath for long, but this looks doable."

The sunshine fell down through the clear blue water causing shadows to ripple and play across the dolphin's gray flanks as they arched over the reef then down to the dead ship below.

"The captain should be keelhauled! What could have possessed him to attempt a crossing in that!" Jasmine asked of no one in particular.

"Okay you two, be alert and be careful!" Bridget said. "The hold is littered with loose rope and we have no human partners with us who could get us loose. If you become entangled, you most likely will not come out. Jasmine I lead, you follow. Marco, you bring up the rear."

"Tail end Charlie again," he muttered to himself. And they slipped inside, single file…

"Oh, by the way… watch out for the dead guy. He gave me quite a scare when I bumped into him," Bridget spoke offhandedly.

"Ooh, gross!" Jasmine said after swimming up close to the ceiling where the corpse floated and scanning it with her sonar.

"Girl, where did you learn words like that? Surely not from me."

Jasmine looked anywhere but at her mother.

"Eyes and ears on the job at hand. There's the air pocket ahead." They surfaced as one, the noise of three dolphins exhaling in a small space was quite loud and they were greeted with a squeal of fright from the two within.

"Fragh! This air is not that good." Marco said.

"You're not Bridget?" The girl asked of the strange voice within the darkness.

"Nope, Marco here, hello!"

Not wanting to be left out, Bridget's daughter bumped Marco in a sensitive spot. The bull flinched away from the unexpected and intimate touch. "Jasmine is here also," Bridget's daughter piped in. "We come to help Bridget. I don't like this place, let's go."

Bridget gave an attention-getting squee. "Listen up everyone, Cory, Jyn, can you hold your breath for a minute or so?"

"Yea, sure, so can my sis. We can swim good too!"

The StarRise pod leader gave a quiet sigh of relief. "That's great kids! It will make this a lot easier. Marco, Jasmine, here are your assignments. Marco, when we go… I want you to station yourself just outside where the hull was breached and stand by to assist if needed. Jas, you'll take the girl… Jyn out first, she is your responsibility. Young ones, are either of you hurt or bleeding?" She asked the two humans. Bridget had visions of trying to fend off bloodsucker fish or other things even worse.

"No Bridget, we're okay. Just a few scratches, but we are so thirsty!"

Bridget replied in sympathy, "Oh, you poor dears, I bet you are! Jas, when you get topside swim down the beach. Inside the reef, there's a stream that enters the lagoon not far away. Marco, when Jas clears the hole, you fall in behind. If Jyn's hand slips, your fin better be there!" The threat was left unspoken. Marco started to move. "Wait! Hear all, then we go." The barge's corpse creaked and moaned then settled around them and dead silence returned once more.

"Okay, okay! This is it, no more time. Marco, they get up, you get back down. Do the same thing for Cory and I. You're on daughter of mine, go Marco!" He disappeared with a splash. "Jyn get in the water with Jasmine and hold on to her fin good! Now take deep fast breaths. When I count to three hold your breath and Jasmine will have you up in no time, trust me."

"I do, Bridget," the girl said with a quiver in her voice.

The fin heard the girl begin to hyperventilate and Bridget started her count… "One… Two… Three!" They were gone and only two remained.

"Just you and me kid." The dolphin tried to make light of the situation, but the dead ship moved around them, the air bubble began shifting and moving dangerously about. "Cory! In the water, now!" There was a splash of a body hitting water and then a hand gripped her dorsal fin hard. "We can't wait for Marco to return, we must go now! Okay, deep breaths, just like your sister… on three."

"Yes, Bridget," he said in a voice tight with fear. The dolphin counted down… and dove into the warm, wet inky blackness.

⇗⇖

Marco swam through the rent in the barge's side and sent a strong sonar pop back to let the three within know he was in position. Marco did not have long to wait until Jasmine came out with the girl holding on with both hands, eyes tightly closed.

He let out a squee of delight, pitching it low in the range of the human ear so the child would hear; he fell in behind Jasmine as backup.

The two dolphins broached side by side, their breaths throwing twin columns of mist into the air. It was then that they both heard the distress call echoing up from below.

Jasmine began to turn, but found her way blocked by Marco's body. "Jas, you know what you must do and where your duty lies, go now! I will see what has happened." With a flick of his tail he dove once more… down to the wreck site below.

⇗⇖

Down under… The world was shifting around her as Bridget swam towards the light streaming through the split in the hull. The ropes were no longer lying on the bottom. They were writhing like living things attempting to ensnare her, but she fought them off.

The dead man danced upon the ceiling as if he were alive once more. Thankfully the boy could see none of it due to the darkness through which they swam. Bridget's head passed through the breach, her mid-body next, the boy was clear…when a tremendous weight descended upon her tail flukes. No matter the amount of threshing, she could not free herself. Bridget was well and truly trapped. She beamed out a distress call and a gray body was there in moments.

"Marco! Take the boy, swim him to safety!"

Marco looked his pod leader in the eye, "Bridget what about…"

Bridget cut him off with a powerful sonar sweep. "No back talk, do as you are told dolphin!!! If ill befalls the man-child, I will come back to haunt you in the sea dream forever!"

Marco knew there was nothing he could do, but no one should die alone. Marco turned with the boy holding his dorsal and went vertical pulling Cory towards the sun and the life-giving air above…

Bridget gave a few more tugs and realized it was futile. This was it then, the end of her life's swim. All that remained was that one last deep dive into the darkness. Bridget slowed her heartbeat to conserve oxygen, why she did not know, but fins did not quit. As long as there is life, there was hope.

She took a moment to compose herself and fight back her fear; Bridget created her sending with care, a wave front of extreme low frequency sound flowed from her into the surrounding sea. Bridget did not have the power of her kin the great humpback whales of old Earth whose booming voices could be heard a half a planet away on the other side of the ocean, but her voice would still travel far, as far as was needed she hoped.

"Fin in danger, fin in distress. Man-children safe, dolphin trapped facing death." Then she waited… but not long. A faint broadcasting reached her in reply to her summons.

"Who, who in danger calls?"

"Bridget, Bridget calls to anyone near. Message the keep and all who can hear, send human with scuba gear."

The return was stronger this time. "Message received, message sent, luck is with us, it is Andy who comes." The transmitting fin was really pushing itself; Bridget estimated a closing speed of twenty knots.

"Who comes?" Bridget asked, a heartbeat went by.

"Ruby comes, to be with her friend. Silence now, save air, your life to extend, you must… Andy will not fail you." Ten to thirteen minutes of life were all that remained… this was going to be a horrible way to die, she thought to herself.

⟋⟍

At the Dolphin Center, same time… "Now just a half turn more… there! That's it." Andy talked to himself, ceasing to tighten the small screws just as the gasket began to squeeze out from the pressure. Giving the regulator a final examination, he reconnected the air hoses and opened the tank valve.

Depressing the small button on the side of the mouthpiece, he heard the satisfying sound of escaping air. Everything was in working order, but he would not trust it until he took it on a shallow test dive.

He noticed that the tank was only half-full and made a mental note to have one of the senior apprentices recharge it and returned the tank to his locker along with his fins and mask.

Andy was about to head out when there arose such a clamor from the dolphin pool, the seaward entrance to the keep that he changed direction to see what was going on.

⟋⟍

It was a clear day. The storm had blown itself out last night and no emergency was in progress, so an apprentice in the junior class was sitting the bell watch. The poor kid nearly had heart failure when the summoning bell erupted in a clamor of sound. Ringing report sequence and emergency almost continuous over and over. The water's surface was being churned into white froth; there were so many fins in the pool.

They were squeeing and whistling in delphin and speaking in the tongue of man, shouting so loudly to be heard that he could not think! The dolphin voices were tumultuous and overlapping. Their squees and whistles reflecting off the stone roof above were deafening in the enclosed space.

The kid was stunned; he had never seen fins act like this! He stood rooted to the spot deciding what he should do, when a bellow of truly impressive proportions issued from the doorway.

⟋⟍

Andy hesitated on his way out, brought up short by the manic ringing of the bell. What was going on down there? He paused in the doorway taking in the chaos. This had to be stopped and stopped now, or they were going to have Commander Trencamp down here and then things would get very ugly indeed!

"Aaatteention!!!" Andy bellowed in a voice used to shouting above the roar of hurricane force winds. The hubbub ceased immediately. "Now! What is going on here?" He spoke in a voice commanding the dolphins' attention and obedience as he strode forward into the cavern to stand on the low stone slab where the dolphins would haul out to be ministered to by the dolphin medics.

Planting hands on hips, Andy glared at the assembled fins. Glancing over at the apprentice, Andy nodded his head. "Lad, you had the right idea, but way too slow. When a situation arises take charge immediately! If you let the fins get wound up, it could take you precious time to restore order, minutes that you may not have, time that could cost a life!" He turned back to regard the crowded pool.

Andy could not be a full-fledged dolphin partner due to his disability. As far as the fins were concerned he was head blind; he could hear not a word of their thoughts. However, the bonding that had taken place on an empty beach between this man and a fin that night in the past was deep and true.

"Now, will someone explain...?" Andy gazed around the pool like a dark cloud looking for someone to throw thunderbolts at. "You there! Speak!"

"Well... I ah. I was..." the dolphin stuttered as it tried to calm itself down and speak clearly.

A small dolphin pushed past the stuttering male and cleared the low sill of the pool's edge to slide across the stone with her head and tail arched away from the slab. She stopped at Andy's feet, her head nodding as she spoke.

"Children of man were in danger, but they were saved. Now the fin is trapped. She asks you to save her, needs air, bring scuba gear."

"Say what?" Andy was as confused as the watch. "Why don't you start over from the beginning...," but the petite dolphin cut him off.

"No time! It's Bridget, you dimwit! She has about ten minutes of air time left."

The eyes of the boy standing next to Andy grew round as the dolphin spoke, "If you don't get a move on your girl is a dead fish! Go, go... GO NOW!!!"

Andy spoke a word and it was not a good one. "Shit!" He turned to leave, but spun back around. "Where?" he asked.

"On the seaward side of the reef, at the bay of the big waves, where you and she like to play."

The small dolphin starred intently at the man as if by shear force of will she might break through the barrier between them. "Hurry, Andy," she whispered at his retreating back. The small female slid tail first into the water.

The room darkened; there was a roaring in his ears. He

turned and ran back to the ready room, shedding clothes as he went. He ripped open his locker snatching up his air tank, swimfins, weight belt, mask and knife before running for the keep's great doors. It was a most unusual sight that was presented to the denizens of the keep. A half-naked man with a scuba tank on his back running away from the water....

⤢⤣

Andy shouted at the pilot of the inter-island shuttle that was about to take off.

"What's up Andy?" The pilot asked.

"Bridget's gone and got herself in trouble, big time! I need you to drop me at the big bay on the other side of the island."

"Hey, do you know what a flight plan is? I can't just go off and...."

"Damn it Rudy, a dolphin's life is at stake!" Andy pointed his finger at the good looking pilot, "And... you owe me. I introduced you to my sister, remember! Look, all you got to do is pull into hover for thirty seconds and I am out the door!"

Rudy threw up his hands as he shook his head, but there was a smile on his face.

"Yea, yea, I can do that. But I am not hangin' around. When you're out the door, I'm gone!"

"Thanks Rudy, I owe you!" Andy shouted above the rising engine whine as the turbines spooled up for liftoff.

⤢⤣

The shuttle climbed into a clear blue sky and flew quickly out to sea. Rudy leaned over and looked back through the open cockpit door at Andy standing next to the cargo hatch. "How will we find the right spot?" he shouted above the roaring turbofans. "One piece of ocean looks like any other more or less!"

"That will not be a problem, look six o'clock low!"

Rudy immediately understood. Two dolphins were leaping out of the water to splash back down creating large white marks on the surface of the sea. He altered course and increased his rate of descent. He pulled the shuttle up into hover flight 30 feet above the waves and began to settle slowly towards the sea surface.

Andy did not wait, he stepped out of the open hatch and holding his facemask in place with one hand, he plunged feet first into the sea.

He entered the water with a splash amid a cloud of bubbles. Andy flipped over and kicked for the bottom. He had not completed the second stroke when a dorsal fin was inserted under his right hand and he was dragged down at a speed no diver alone could have matched.

Tilting his head sideways, Andy exhaled through his nose to clear the water from his mask. Looking through the glass clear water Andy took in the scene below, the upturned hull and the ledge on which it rested so perilously close to the brink. Then he saw her and his breath caught momentarily in his throat. To see the other woman in his life so close to freedom, but unable to escape to the air above tore at his very soul... he had to do something! Glancing up he realized just how shallow the wreck site was, he guessed a little over 20 feet at the most. The dolphin continued pulling him downward, closer to his friend.

Bridget lay motionless, fighting a desperate life or death battle with her own body... and she was losing! Tiny bubbles were beginning to leak past the sphincters that held her blowhole closed. It had been a good thirteen minutes since Bridget had taken her last breath of air. Some fin had once told her that drowning was not a bad way to die... once you got over the terror at the beginning, that is. It still sounded like sick humor to her, but she was going to find out first hand; it would not be long now.

Bridget's vision was going black around the edges. Her lungs felt as if there was a fire burning her from within. Why not relax, let the cool seawater fill her lungs and end the burning pain? Bubbles began to escape from her blowhole once more.

"Click, squee!"

She had been hearing white noise for some time, but was too preoccupied with the internal struggle to understand the sound of speech. But it was drawing closer, now it was beside her.

"Mother... mother? Mother!!! Come out of the sea dream, I have brought him as you asked. Please, talk to us!"

Andy wasted no time once Jasmine had brought him to her mother's side. Running his hands down her flanks produced only a mild tremor, Bridget was still unaware of the outside world.

Desperate situations call for desperate measures. Sliding his hands rearwards along the fin's body he located her mammary glands, which on a dolphin female are concealed within two slits on her underbelly.

Taking the cow's teats between forefingers and thumbs he squeezed them cruelly. The sharp bright pain from an unexpected quarter did the trick. The dark eyes that the man had looked into that first night in the past to see the person within now lost the glazed look that had scared Andy so when Jasmine brought him down to where her mother lay trapped on the sea floor.

With Bridget alert and focused, Andy held his breath, removed the scuba mouthpiece and snapped on the air-dome. Slapping it over her blowhole he gave her the hand signal to blow. The long held breath was released, exploding from her blowhole and purging the water from the dome. Bridget pulled in a deep draft of air of life itself. She held it just long enough for a good O_2/CO_2 exchange exhaled again and took another deep breath.

Her man replaced the mouthpiece between his lips and took a breath himself. He then returned it to her once more, buddy breathing. They repeated the cycle again until Bridget had removed the excess carbon dioxide from her bloodstream.

With the immediate danger being past, Andy slid his hand towards her tail. Beyond the barge's hull his hand encountered something massive that he could not move, try as he might.

Jasmine nudged Andy to get his attention and gestured towards the surface. The twin hulls of a small fast catamaran could be seen slicing through the water above.

It was becoming difficult to draw air from the scuba tank; Andy knew what it meant. He had no choice. Swimming close to Bridget he mounted the air-dome onto the mouthpiece once more, covered her blowhole and gave her the proper hand signal. Bridget blew once, twice… then shook her head side to side. Andy replaced the mouthpiece and sucked hard, a mere gust of air came out at his demand. It was time to go; there was nothing more he could do.

He broke the surface and held onto the hull of the catamaran just as the two men aboard dropped into the water.

"How's she doing Andy?" one of them asked.

"Not good. Whatever has her tail pinned was too heavy for me to move. I could not get her free."

"Well, we will just see about that." He glanced at the crow-bar clutched in his hand and without another word took hold of the dolphin's fin and it pulled him below the surface.

The other was about to go under, but paused as Andy spoke. "Kelly, her life is in your hands...." Emotion filled his words and he was almost unable to speak. "If, if you can't free her... you know what must be done." Andy drew his knife and passed it over to the man who took it with a hand that shook as he realized what he might have to do.

Kelly glanced down at the blade in his hand, then slipped it into the empty sheath upon his leg. He looked Andy in the eye. "I understand." The killer placed a hand upon his friend's shoulder. "I swear to you Andy, if there is no other way, it will be quick and clean, she won't even know she is dead... I will strike at the base of the skull where...."

"Enough!!! Speak no more about it!" Andy shouted in horror. "Just! ...just do the deed and have done with it...," Andy whispered as he turned away.

"Don't give up hope Andy, she hasn't." His friend pulled down his mask and dove for the wreck below.

Andy leaned his head against the side if the boat and inhaled the fresh salt-laden air. His tears fell unheeded to mix with and disappear into the sea.

A dolphin broached silently behind him and listened for a few moments to the sound of the man crying. Then swimming to him, she nudged Andy gently with her beak. "Do not cry Andy, she is not dead yet. Your friends fight for you and they will not give up easily," Jasmine said.

Andy reached out to Bridget's daughter and held her tightly. "What will I do, Jasmine, if they fail?"

"You will do the same as I... you will go on," she replied and began to pull Andy deeper into the bay.

"What are you doing, Jas?"

"I'm taking you where you are needed." The dolphin swam on in silence.

☇☈

Twenty feet down the fight continued. The two divers tore at the rotten hull planks with their crowbars. Bridget stoically bore it all lying motionless, conserving the breath she had for there would be no more.

With a groaning accompanied by the creaking pops of over-stressed timber, the dead barge slid from the sand-covered ledge and soared out over the abyss.

It hovered momentarily, as if unsure which direction to go. Then it began the final plunge down into the depths below, taking two more down with it.

Kelly redoubled his efforts, but it was futile. He knew the moment of decision had come. *Forgive me Bridget. I give you the only gift I have... a quick death.*

The dolphin nodded its head as the man's thoughts came into her mind.

He drew Andy's knife from the sheath strapped to his leg. The blade flickered coldly in the waning light as the barge sank towards the bottom so far below; Kelly drew back his arm for the thrust that would kill Andy's friend....

The thoughts that gently touched his mind were ones he rarely experienced. He cherished them, enjoying their sparkling newness and femininity that was so different from Archer's male-ness. He was saddened that the person who had created them would be lost to him.

Tell Andy that I love him...

Kelly blinked in surprise, *I will...*

He knew that he would feel Bridget's death for the rest of his life. For the link he and all dolphin partners shared with the Sea People would carry her dying into his very soul, but he hard-ened his heart knowing it was the right thing to do...and his hand slipped upon the moss covered hull. Without thought he stabbed the knife blade deep into the wood to keep from being torn away from the sinking barge, there-by dooming the trapped dolphin to a horrible death as the pressure built until at last the life was crushed from her body.

The barge began to oscillate as it sank downwards. The wa-ter darkened and turned cold around them as they fell farther and farther away from the world of life and light.

Bridget felt the scow begin to swing from side to side, using her flippers she was able to keep from being banged against the hull. Then without warning the weight lifted from her tail and the dolphin squirted free like a melon seed squeezed from between a man's

fingers. She reached deep into herself and stroked for the surface with the last of her strength holding nothing back, for it was now or never, life or death.

Kelly watched the dolphin swim upwards towards a surface. *That's it friend of my friend, swim to the light!*

He willed the dolphin to swim on, but around the man, it was dark and the water was like liquid ice against his skin. Wrenching the knife free was turning out to be no easy task. But free it did come at last.

He kicked his feet and followed Bridget at a more leisurely pace allowing his natural buoyancy to bring him once more to the surface.

She began to blow just shy of the surface. Breaking into the clear air, the remainder of her last breath rushed from her blowhole at over ninety miles an hour. The whole cycle took less than three tenths of a second and she splashed back down into the water to lie motionless upon the sea. Bridget floated at the surface, content just to breathe until at last the shaking of her pectoral fins had stopped....

⟰⟱

Same time inside the bay... The sandy bottom shoaled up to where Andy could at last touch it with his feet. He released his hold upon the dolphin's fin and walked out onto the strand. Removing tank, mask and weight belt, he leaned them against a fallen log under a great tree, well above the high tide mark.

"Jyn, Cory!" the dolphin called, followed by a loud squee whistle.

Andy turned upon hearing the sound to see Jasmine standing on her tail to get a better view. Due to the design of a dolphin's eye they had excellent binocular vision in and out of the water, as well as monocular vision when underwater. Also like man, their retinas contained both rods and cones allowing them to see in color. She splashed back into the water only to bob back up a moment later.

Marco says go up the stream. They are on the bank where the water turns fresh.

What am I thinking, he can't hear me! Jasmine berated herself, for a moment she had forgotten that Andy was head blind. Well, he may not be able to hear my thoughts, but he can hear my voice! "Hey Andy! Marco says go up the stream. They are on the bank where the water turns fresh."

Jasmine swam up the stream a short distance, then returned. The fresh water felt strange against her skin.

Andy gave the hand sign for understanding. "Thanks sweetheart!" Following her directions he soon spotted small footprints in the stream bank that guided him quickly to the ones he sought.

Andy caught sight of them sitting on a large bough overhanging the water. It was high enough to keep them safe from prowling beasts and they could slip off of it to land in the waters of the stream next to the dolphin that would swim them to safety, if needed.

"Hola! You kids all right?" He crossed the clearing towards the children who quickly came down from the tree where they had taken refuge and ran towards him.

"Are you Andy, the deaf guy?" The girl asked.

The man smiled. "Well, my name is Andy and I am as deaf as a post as far as the dolphins are concerned," he tapped his temple with a forefinger. "Yep, must be me!"

He turned to the dolphin in the stream and with a few hand signs told him to return to the sea. Sign language was, in truth, unnecessary to communicate with the Sea People, but it was a holdover from long ago and to this day all dolphins and those humans that wished to partner with them learned it.

Andy returned his attention to the two children who stood looking expectantly at him.

"Well, you two do not look too much the worse for your ordeal, but we'll get you to the keep and let medical have a look at you just to make sure and then we will see about getting you home."

"The boat was our home," the boy said.

Andy was taken aback for a moment, "Oh, I see," was all he could think of as he realized that he most likely had a pair of orphans on his hands.

"Where's Bridget?" the girl child asked as they walked out on to the beach. The smile upon his face disappeared.

At the same instant Jasmine cried out. The man had never heard a fin make such a distressing sound.

I am sorry Andy… they tried.

Archer's thoughts were so full of sorrow they hit Andy like a hammer blow and he fell to his knees. "Oh no, Bridget! No my love, oh please no…."

She is free! She is free! Bridget rises!

"Yes!" he shouted while leaping to his feet once more. His joy and relief were so great that he did not even realize that Archer had not spoken a word. The stress of the moment had cracked the barrier within Andy's mind.

The significance of the moment did not escape the dolphin's quick bright mind. Archer would tell the others and together they would attack the barrier until at last it would fall before the force of their combined wills. Then Andy would truly be one of them.

The kids had stepped back, giving the madman plenty of room. Maybe there was some truth to the stories their father had told them about the humans who swam with dolphins.

Seeing the looks on their faces Andy reigned in his emotions.

Jyn looked at him and cocked her head sideways. "Do you always act like that when a dolphin talks to you? Our dad says that the dolphin folk are weird, especially when it comes to sex…."

Andy almost missed a step. "Well, to answer your question, no I don't… it's just that Bridget is someone I am very close to. I would miss her if she were gone and I was so happy when she got free that I just had to shout about it… and what do you know about sex! I mean, how old are you…twelve, thirteen?"

With hands on hips she replied, "I'll have you know that I am a full fourteen years old! And we barge rats grow up fast." Andy took note of the points of her budding womanhood. "I see," was his only reply once more….

The conversation had taken them to the water's edge. The two dolphins greeted them with squees, whistles and other happy sounds, coming as close to the beach as they dared.

"As soon as we return to the keep I will notify the proper authority and they will get a search party up to see if there are other survivors. Hopefully your parents will be among them." The girl's reaction took him completely by surprise.

"If I ever see the bastard again it'll be too soon! May he rot in Davie Jones' locker and be eaten by the fishes!"

Andy glanced sharply at the young girl who had her head down in shame. Andy understood in a flash what had caused her outburst and his blood grew hot. The scut of a man had the gall to name dolphins and their partners perverted? Bastard indeed!

Just then a loud commotion drew Andy's attention to the water, where a troika of happy fins leaped out of the water with joy at the return of one they thought gone. "Bridget's here!" he said to no one in particular and broke into a run towards the water.

Without slacking pace he entered it, water splashing in all directions. He dove in, cleaving through the small waves and stroked powerfully towards his friends. He was quickly included in their antics being rubbed, nuzzled and dunked until he had, for his own safety, reached for the whistle that hung around his neck.

The chaos subsided and the threesome parted to let the fourth dolphin swim past. Bridget swam slowly towards her man. Stopping at arm's length she drank in the sight of him, committing every line and curve of his face and body to memory. She knew Andy in ways that no women of his own species would ever know him. His clothes hid nothing from her sight; neither did his skin.

Bridget slid forward through the water to lean her melon against his chest; she could hear and see the heart within beating strongly.

It skipped a beat as Andy cupped her beak in his hand and tenderly brought the other arm around her to hug Bridget tightly to him. A heavy sigh of contentment escaped her blowhole.

"Bridget, my love, I thought I had lost you!" Andy spoke. His voice was tight with emotion.

The man's words rocked the dolphin to her core. They were words she had dreamed of hearing from his lips, but dared not to hope. Others had said the chasm was too wide, the one who attempts the leap was sure to have their heart broken. But love is like starlight, a universal constant. It does not recognize gender or species. It just is and always will be.

I love you also, Andy, she thought, knowing that her words went unheard. Bridget touched his lips with her beak. *I kiss my chosen, to thank him in the old way for my life once more.*

As she spoke Andy was running his hands over her body assuring himself that she was truly okay, his touch sending flashes of pleasure through her sensitive skin. She could not deny her feelings, or the emotions his touch roused within her.

The dolphin satisfied herself with a quick sonar scan and nuzzle of his body while her partner (for that is what he was; she did not care that he could not hear her) examined her tail.

Luckily for Bridget, dolphin's tail flukes are flattened pads of tough, dense fibrous connective tissue, completely without bone or muscle. Her flukes had several new nicks in the trailing edge, but the vessels had sealed and there was no bleeding to attract predators.

Andy released her tail and Bridget's head popped up. "You feel up to the swim back?" he asked. Her only response was a disdainful fountain of water from her blowhole.

Bridget turned her back, Andy flashed a hand sign at the other three fins and they crowded close. "Look," he spoke in a low voice. "I want you three to watch her close," he said, as his hands moved. At the first sign of distress, you send for us and we'll fly her back. Got it?" He reached out and tapped each up-turned beak as he spoke. The trio nodded their heads in unison.

"She's not gonna like that," Ruby commented.

"In this case, I don't really care what she happens to like or doesn't like," Jasmine said. "Bridget was almost lost to me the day Andy saved her and was nearly taken from me again today! I will not lose my mother because of dolphin pride... that I-can-swim-around-the-world-and-not-get-tired crap! Watch over her with me, my friends." That brought on more head-shaking and then they too swam off, following their pod leader home.

It was not long until the catamaran hove into view. Andy tossed his gear onboard. The two children climbed on and he pushed the small craft out away from the beach. He pulled himself aboard and leaned back against the mainmast.

Kelly reached down, pulling Andy's knife from the sheath upon his leg. He looked at it for a long moment, realizing how close he had come to having to do the unthinkable. With a flick of the wrist, he reversed the knife and passed the big blade to Andy hilt first.

Bridget's partner took his knife back and placed it in its sheath once more. "Kelly, thank you for accepting the duty. When the moment comes and the choice must be made, it takes a strong man to give mercy."

Kelly took a deep breath and sighed. "It's a choice I pray I will never have to make again, Andy." He turned away and looked out to sea. The clouds blazed with color as the sun sank below the horizon into a fiery twilight. The catamaran's sails were set and adjusted. Then together, dolphins and men made their way back to the keep.

L. J. Anderson

L.J. Anderson was raised on the small eighty-acre Anderson family farm in the agricultural community of Blythe, California. After finishing high school, where he acquired a love for reading, he enlisted in the United States Navy and served his country overseas. Upon his discharge, his traveled about the country for several years before returning once more to his home in the Palo Verde Valley. While working as a farm equipment specialist by day, he nurtured his proclivity towards fantasy writing at night as a way to relax after a hard day's work and was soon addicted to expressing his fascination in a fantasy world of his own creation. He lives in Blythe with his wife Kathy, their nine-year-old son Riley and a white honey-dipped Labrador Retriever named Xena. This is his second appearance in the CrossTIME Science Fiction Anthology.

A Friend in Need...
Richard O. C. Cousens

The Emperor Vogdane died as the ship departed. He tried his best to remain conscious during the dedication and blessing of the mighty vessel, but the virus finally overwhelmed him as the vectoring thrusters fired. They aligned the ship with its projected course — placed its heading on the path that would carry a most precious cargo far beyond the limits of their worked-out galaxy.

Even before the main propulsion drive jetted its ionised trail for the first time, Vogdane's body was unceremoniously cremated and ejected into space. His sticklike limbs and long, fragile bodyshell burned briefly before disappearing from view in the blackness outside. There could be no possibility of contamination, even with as illustrious a being as Vogdane himself. His ashes would circle Gardaar for eternity, scattered widely by the little shuttle's blast as it headed back to the surface.

The launch had been successful. The massive craft was on its way — it was up to the gods now as to whether it would find a suitable world to deposit its cargo and so re-establish the Gardaarian race.

As the shuttle headed back to Gardaar City, the mood was sombre. The navigator was silent at his console and the High Priest and his entourage didn't attempt to distract him with conversation. They had none to offer anyway. The cargo had been blessed and that was the end of their involvement in the affair.

Deep within the ship now heading out into space, the support systems were activated; all conscious beings had left on the last shuttle returning to Gardaar. The next activity would be at the end of the voyage, millions of cycles in the future. Everyone realised that long before then Gardaarians would be extinct here — their hopes for the future rested with the cargo being exported.

Although most of the ship's interior was not illuminated, the highly protected section in the centre of the vessel was in semi-darkness, lit only by infra-red heaters keeping the chill of deep space at bay. Row upon row of glistening blue eggs lay in their protective cocoons, constantly monitored, waiting for the moment that would herald a new dawn for the Gardaarian race. They had been carefully selected and screened for the virus before being packed into their cushioned shelters.

A variety of seeds and plant matter had been crammed in mini-ecopods with the egg cocoons, to be ejected into the surrounding area once a suitable destination had been located. The onboard computers were programmed to seek a planet with the correct combination of temperature, atmospheric composition, surface liquid and gravity for their potential new home.

The latest virus had taken a severe toll in a very short space of time. The inherent Gardaarian genetic flaw had allowed the spread of this latest plague to run almost unchecked through the population, leaving a relative handful alive. Their present hosts, a sturdy race from a system far out on the rim of the galaxy, had been their last chance for survival, and now the symbiotic relationship they had enjoyed for thousands of generations had failed them.

The weakness manifested itself once again, and it was necessary to find a new host. This galaxy had been scoured clean of potential symbiotic partners over the millennia, necessitating the construction of the biggest single craft ever built.

Their present elongated physical form had a lot to do with the current host race. Even though the Gardaarians seldom absorbed more than half the characteristics of a host, there was no record of what the original Gardaarian looked like. The prototype had existed so long ago that its true nature was lost in the mists of time. But as long as a single Gardaarian gene existed, the race was alive.

↗↘

Silently, the huge ship carried its cargo out of the dense cluster of stars that had been home and into the void of deep space. Its passage was unmarked for millions of Gardaarian cycles, the only activity being the occasional mobilisation of swarms of hulldrones attending to meteorite damage. Otherwise, time may well have stood still for the ship and its cargo as it drifted slowly, silently across the emptiness, heading inexorably into a distant spiral nebula, until an alarm activated in the Control Area.

There was no conscious being on board; no life form was awake to take notice. Instead, ancient computed options and instructions came into play, and the long silent thrusters fired briefly, bringing the ship onto a new heading. The scanners had detected a blue and white planet orbiting a minor sun out in one of the spiral's arms that appeared suitable, and adjusted course accordingly.

The unborn Gardaarians were almost at the end of their voyage. The giant vessel was not designed to land on a planet. It was too massive; it would have been torn apart by gravitational stresses and burnt up on entry into a thick atmosphere, and so the computers guided it to a safer destination. They selected the single moon orbiting the planet. The ship touched down safely on the side facing away from its new potential home.

The aeons-long silence was well and truly broken, and a section of the ship slid aside, allowing the cargo compartment, complete with propulsion system and auto-guidance controls, to slide clear and blast off for its final destination. The modified shuttle penetrated the heavy atmosphere of the watery planet, selected a suitable looking landmass and landed heavily in a swamp, inadvertently wiping out a small herd of ungainly reptilian beasts browsing on the heavy foliage of a steamy forest.

It sank quickly below the surface, and the safety systems locked the exits in place, waiting for a clearance signal from the sensors on the hull surface. As the shuttle was submerged, no signal was given, and in time the land was rocked by violent geological activity and the swamp dried. Fault lines cracked apart and huge sections of ground collapsed. The shuttle was enveloped by a flow of lava from a nearby volcano. It remained buried below layers of igneous and later sedimentary matter, for millions more cycles, until a team of geologists, drilling cores for a projected tunnel below a seaway linking two land masses, found bits of an unknown alloy and broken eggshells in their samples.

A team of analysts in their mobile laboratory wasted no time in determining that these shells were no fossils — they were from live, unhatched eggs, and when the transport tunnel was finally excavated, a small diversionary offshoot was dug to investigate the find more closely.

In their wildest dreams, the team of scientists who brought the discovery to the surface would never have imagined the consequences of this action.

As the layer in which the discovery was found belonged to the Cretaceous period, the containers and their precious contents were taken across an ocean to the laboratory of the foremost palaeontologist of the day. That was where the cocoons' monitoring devices calculated that conditions were just right for hatching, and the world was never the same again.

༄༅

"Look at the little things — aren't they just the cutest?" Barbara Westville was watching a pair of juvenile hatchlings trying to climb a small bush in the sealed laboratory nursery. The seeds accompanying the eggs grew into plants that thrived, so much so that the botanists running the nursery side of it had daily to cut back a huge amount of vegetation. It threatened to engulf the domed half-acre under cultivation. There was no species of flora on Earth that could match it for speed of growth and adaptation to differing conditions.

They experimented with various combinations of heat, humidity and water, or lack of it, and the foliage appeared the same within a matter of days, no matter whether the plant was in swampy or desert conditions. It adapted so swiftly that the scientists were alarmed, and more stringent quarantine structures were put in place. The danger of these plants spreading into the outside world and overwhelming the planet was very real.

"They may look cute, my dear, but their incredibly swift growth is what worries me," Professor Milton Rhodes commented as he stood watching the antics of the little stick insect-like creatures.

"It's far in excess of anything on this planet. I really don't think they belong. They're certainly not from the Cretaceous — I'd be really surprised if they're from here at all. This is an alien life form — I'm convinced of it. The analysts couldn't identify the alloy used in the containers. Quite how they got to be buried so deeply is a puzzle. But the rate of growth — it's so rapid it worries the hell out of me." He shook his head gently, clucking quietly. Barbara was the only one he ever confided in as far as the alien theory was concerned. He didn't want to dent his credibility by making his suspicions public — not just yet. Let them keep assuming they were species of prehistoric insect and flora growing in there.

He shook his head again, peering closer at one of the little creatures. It seemed to notice and stared back at him.

"Yes, it worries me all right. That and their genetic makeup. We've analysed their DNA, identified the collective genome and discovered a number of genetic markers. I'm pretty sure their cells contain strands of unrelated DNA. There's been a history of gene transfer in there that doesn't add up at all. I think these cute little fellows are part of a symbiotic lifestyle that has somehow gone wrong. Their genetic makeup is flawed — they have no resistance to even the slightest hostile virus, as you've noted."

"Well, these last two seem to be surviving, Professor," Barbara said quietly. "So far, so good. The new isolation barriers in place seem to be effective. The earlier casualties were so disappointing, weren't they? We tried so hard, but even the tiniest slip and some organism would find its way into the nursery. The poor little things didn't stand a chance against our bugs. From the very beginning, we had the most stringent isolation techniques available in place, but it wasn't enough, was it? But Professor, if we manage to keep these two, what's to become of them? Could we ever let them out of here?" she asked, sweeping her arm to encompass the glass-fronted viewing area where they stood. Her blonde hair swung across her high cheekbones as her head moved with the action.

Professor Rhodes, his thinning sandy hair falling untidily across his high forehead, peered into her deep blue eyes. As always, he was gratified to rediscover the mixture of beauty and brains that validated sponsoring his delightful protégéé. Barbara was as intelligent as she was good-looking, and her charming but no-nonsense manner captivated all who worked here at the experimental laboratory set up under his guidance when the eggs were first discovered.

"If we manage to bring these two to adulthood, my dear, we'll have to see about reproduction — so far they appear to be asexual. I suspect the symbiotic relationship they had previously may have altered their reproductive cycle. I want to start exposing them to local life forms sometime later. We'll have to wait and see. In the meantime, we'll keep on observing. For now, just keep them isolated." He smiled and moved off, away from the steamy tropical kindergarten for alien creatures; the first on the planet, he was proud to claim. To himself anyway.

⚭⚭

Halfway down a service alleyway at the side of the huge isolation area, Matt Lusted and Wilma Devarr were sitting having coffee. The rest facility was a recent innovation — Professor Rhodes had taken pity on the support staff who worked long hours servicing the fast-growing botanic garden that was the alien nursery, and installed a vending machine for them so that they wouldn't have to walk halfway across the vast complex at each designated break period.

"Those last two dead ones we removed yesterday — you remember how the one seemed to twitch a few times before we got it through the tunnel to the dissection lab?" Matt asked.

"Mmm. Little creature jerked a bit — I thought it was some sort of delayed reaction, Matt. The Prof assured us it was dead, but apparently it revived. Why do you ask?"

"Well, when we got it to the lab, I noticed a little cut, here on my wrist," he pulled up the sleeve of his coverall and revealed a red welt across the skin surrounding a small abrasion.

"Looks like it's infected. You'd better get it seen to, buddy," Wilma commented. "Never know with that foreign stuff growing in there. Even with this personal protective gear there's always the chance that something will get through. Does it hurt?"

"Nah — just a scratch. Itches a bit."

"Well, you'd better get it seen to anyway. Can't take chances."

"Yeah, I guess you're right. I'll go see the medic after this shift. Come on, we'd better get to it — only a couple hours to go," he sighed, getting to his feet.

He stood for a moment, rocking gently as the scenery around him seemed to waver and blur, and then moved off slowly, following Wilma. Their next task would be to remove the excess growth cut earlier, out through the isolation tunnel. They would have to don new protective material for that.

He and Wilma both sighed as they reached the decontamination area. So much time wasted each break — discarding their used gear and donning fresh equipment. Still, they simply couldn't take a chance — the big bugs inside there wouldn't last long if any potential contaminant was introduced, and they sure didn't want to be held responsible for anything that serious.

Walking behind his companion, Matt swayed, clutching for support as his vision blurred once more. He resolved to go directly to see the medics the moment his shift was over. But he didn't make it there. He fell into a ditch at the side of the car park on his way out and it was four days before anyone discovered him. By then it was too late for anything the medics could do. He had already begun to exhibit signs of growing compound eyes and a shell-like covering was emerging from the top of his spine.

⚐⚐

Todd Barkhuizen stood at the edge of a cliff and surveyed the jungle below. What had once been a sprawling suburb, with streets, schools, shopping malls, churches and row upon row of houses was now completely swamped by the virulent growth that escaped from that damned scientific research centre. Not only the flora, but rumour had it that the prehistoric insect-like creatures they'd seen on TV recently had also escaped and were even now spreading through the area, causing panic among the frightened populace.

He looked along the dark, jagged stripe bisecting the flat ground in front of him. Damned stupid place to build a sensitive laboratory — right next to a fault line like that. That heavy 'quake five days ago had brought down the nursery section and nobody had seen those strange little prehistoric insect creatures again. And as for the plant life that was rapidly taking over the area — it was spreading at the rate of one city block per day. In no time at all the city would be covered as well, if they didn't do something very quickly.

He shook his head again, trying to get rid of the feeling that something was calling him. For days now, he'd had the weirdest dreams and even when he was awake, strange thoughts kept intruding. It was as if someone was trying to communicate with him.

He shrugged the feeling off and turned to his Jeep. This place was a potential disaster anyway — too crowded for him. Why he ever left his desert home he couldn't imagine. The lure of better prospects had soured very quickly when he really got down to it. City life was not for him. He climbed in and started the engine, heading onto the highway for home, far away from this giant, freewheeling lunatic asylum, to where the air was clean and the land was open.

The little floral hitchhiker, clinging to the instep of his rugged boot, went with him all the way; ready to start a new colony of foliage in a drier land that would soon resemble the creeping green tide below the cliff he'd just left.

ろ卍

"We can't just keep on killing them, Major. They're half human, for Christ's sake," the young, fuzz-headed Private spat a thin stream of tobacco juice.

"You got a better idea, Fitts?" Major Leroy Curtis asked belligerently. "Those are bugs, whether they got human heads or legs or whatever. Bugs, got it? And the only good bug is a dead bug, far as I'm concerned. Until I'm told otherwise, these parasites are the enemy and our job is to kill the enemy, right?"

"Yeah right, Major." Private Travis Fitts moved aside as his partner stuck his head out of the tank turret and surveyed the scene. Turning to the Officer, he spoke out in a loud voice.

"Come on, Major, surely there must be some other way. Jeez, we've killed maybe a thousand today alone, and they still keep coming. They don't fight back. And that last lot — Major, they had faces that looked like people I know. I can't keep burning faces I know like this. It's getting to me. One of them looked like my roomie at Varsity. Hell, I felt like I was killing my buddy there."

"Ah crap, Maitland. You college kids got too much imagination, that's your trouble. Those scientist guys keep telling us these bugs assimilate humans or something. They're goddam parasites — that's why they look like that. Lookit, they're not human, buddy."

"They don't assimilate people, Major, nor are they parasites. They live in symbiosis. They took humans initially and used them as hosts — but they adapt on their own as time goes by.

They evolve constantly and very rapidly, changing the genetic structure to suit themselves and-"

"Yeah, yeah, if you say so. They're still the enemy and until I say so, you take them out, understood?"

"Yes, Major," Private Maitland said quietly as the next column of conscripts arrived to join them in the sweep of the outer city limits.

They found another nest of the creatures, but Private Harold Maitland found no pleasure in torching the squealing, half human-half insect things that curled up and popped as their encased thoraxes swelled and blew apart in the intense heat.

They'd managed to dispose of nearly two thousand by the end of the day, but that would hardly dent what was to come.

ᘔᔦ

As the sun set on yet another horrific day of carnage and stink, Barbara Westville stood on the sundeck of her beachfront home staring out to sea. The noise of the last few days had thankfully subsided. The screams of terrified people charging about killing the hordes of frightening creatures, looking like a scene from some horror movie was over. It was quiet now. The only sounds came from distant chainsaws clearing thick vegetation from the streets and power lines it had choked.

The revelation that the Jesuit Priest sitting in her living room had managed to communicate with the hybrid creatures infesting most of the western seaboard had come as a shock. Not so much that he was capable of telepathy — there were more cases of people demonstrating this newfound talent every day; it was the feedback that he imparted to her.

The 'bugs' were not inherently aggressive creatures, but their aeons-long survival instincts had been honed to such an extent that they didn't consider their actions at all. All that mattered was survival of the species at any cost, and as quickly as possible as far as obtaining and modifying the DNA of new hosts was concerned.

They had no intention of deliberately harming humans, according to Brother Emmanuel. Difficult as it seemed, she believed it. The fact that humanity was suffering badly from the shock of the initial assimilation and subsequent invasion by these alien life forms did little to reassure her, but she accepted his words.

The aliens were telepathic. This much she already suspected. They seemed to know instinctively when harm was about to be put their way. Contrary to popular belief, they had never actually attacked or deliberately harmed a human, at least to her knowledge, apart from the mysterious death and subsequent deformity of that lab nursery worker. However, their process of ultra swift incorporation of human DNA into their genetic structure coupled with an incredibly short period of gestation — clutches of eggs would be laid a few days apart with no contact with each other observed — led to a virtual swamping of the area inhabited by humans.

The babies were fully functional at hatching, and grew at an alarming rate as they fed off the equally fast growing alien vegetation. Within a few days they appeared to be fully grown. The really disturbing thing about them, though, was their increasingly bizarre appearance.

Mixing genes with humans resulted in a variety of shapes and sizes. The earlier ones resembled the original hatchling closely — long, thin and more like a praying mantis than anything else; a wide head with compound, multi-faceted eyes on either side, and a mouth where mandibles would have been. Their long claws had evolved to be highly flexible and they were amazingly delicate in their actions.

At the other end of the spectrum were hybrids that resembled deformed humans from a nightmare gone wrong. Short, squat bodied creatures with long, clawed hands and humanoid faces on bony, shell-like heads generated instant revulsion and fear among the humans they encountered, with the usual result; the halfbreed would be killed mercilessly.

Barbara moved back into the living room where the young priest was shuffling through some papers. He looked up at her.

"Look, we must talk about this in depth. It's against all God's laws to take life, even if it's only half human, and taking it indiscriminately, which is what's happening here," Brother Emmanuel said quietly as she rejoined him. Sipping her wine, she studied the young man for a while before replying.

He was tall, fair haired and green-eyed, and below the ill-fitting clothes he evidently had the build of a gymnast. Pity about his vocation, she thought to herself. He would be an interesting catch, if he was available.

"Brother, you say you're telepathic. Have you always been so?"

"No. It's a fairly recent occurrence, although our Foundation in the desert has been studying the phenomenon for well over a century. We've always been convinced of its existence, but lately, since the discovery of those eggs in fact, it's become a very swiftly growing fact of life. We think it has something to do with the aliens, for that's what they are, isn't it?" he asked, his penetrating green eyes staring at her questioningly.

Barbara didn't reply — she didn't have to. He knew it was so. She shifted uncomfortably.

He continued. "I've communicated with a number of them, and they want nothing more than to be left to live. The problem they have is that they cannot survive on their own — they must have a symbiotic host, and at the moment we're it. Nothing can stand in the way of this fact — they must find a host immediately when arriving on a new world, and they found one here. They're experimenting with differing ratios of human and their own genes to find the most successful combination for the present. That's the gist of what I understood from them. They don't speak, exactly — it was more a series of images flashing across my mind."

"So, what do you suggest, Brother? That we let them continue to corrupt the human species, breed uncontrollably and take over the planet? Because that's exactly what they seem to be doing. Inadvertently perhaps, but it doesn't help us, does it?"

The Jesuit was silent for a while. Barbara noticed him staring at her glass, and she suddenly realised she was merely assuming he didn't drink alcohol.

"Would you like a glass?" she asked, holding up hers.

"Thought you'd never ask," he laughed.

They moved out onto the sundeck to watch the last scarlet tipped spears rising from the western horizon to pierce the low clouds drifting in from the ocean. The sun's final rays died and the world grew more still.

"Never tire of watching the Lord's wonders, do we humans?" he said quietly after a while.

Barbara turned to him and smiled. He wasn't bad looking either, she decided. She toyed idly with the idea of trying to unconvert him.

"Humans being the operative word in this context, Brother. What's your real name? Not your Saint's name; the one you were baptised?"

"Ah, but that would be telling," he answered, a soft Irish brogue slipping through for the first time. He was visibly more relaxed after the first few sips of wine.

She studied him for a moment, then got back to the subject at hand.

"All right then, Brother Emmanuel. I've contacted the foremost geneticist we know. Professor Rhodes is a close colleague of his, in fact. They studied at Oxford together. Anyway, he's on his way over to join us. Professor Graham Hynes should be here later this evening. I'd like you to join us, if you would."

"Join you? Doing what?"

"Observing. We think we have the key to what ails the alien species. They apparently have a flaw in their genetic makeup and we think we know where it lies."

"And what can you do about it?"

"Firstly, we can assist Professor Hynes in determining if our theory is correct, and then begin gene therapy. If all goes well, we may have a genetically sound alien ready within a short space of time. As you know, their reproductive cycle is very rapid, which will be a great help."

"Playing God? Altering the genetic structure of any—"

"Oh for goodness' sake, Brother! Don't pontificate. We're rectifying a wrong, not causing harm. In fact, we'll be doing both species a big favour, so don't get all—"

"Mistress Barbara —"

"Don't Mistress me, Brother. I'm nobody's mistress," she flashed at him. She was feeling frustrated, not only by the way the conversation was going.

"I only meant to say that the result of tampering with genes is all around us right now — the terrible looking aliens resulting from that meddling is evidence that it's against all God's laws to interfere with —"

"Crap. Mankind's been doing it for decades and to the benefit of the human race, so I'm not really interested. You show me where God wrote that we shouldn't improve the species if we can. Look, do you want to get involved or not?"

"I would prefer you not to go ahead, of course, but as you obviously intend to, I would appreciate observing," he said lamely.

She crossed the deck into the living room. It was getting chilly out there, and the wine was inside anyway. They sat together in the darkening room, each thinking very different thoughts about how the next few days would be.

Slowly, she became aware that the young man sitting across the room was thinking of the creatures. She could feel his compassion for their predicament, and the more she felt his thoughts, the more she could feel their pain. It was as if she was tuning in to them en masse. She looked at Brother Emmanuel and he looked back at her, nodding slowly.

Outside, some nearby flame throwers hissed and lit the sky briefly, heralding a fresh clutch of either eggs or juveniles going up in smoke. All the adults, the bizarre and the not too awful examples had been rooted out and disposed of. Only the nests they left behind were posing a threat now. The combined might of the joint Armed Forces and Police had cleaned them out.

The good Brother shuddered and raised his glass once more. This could be an interesting exercise, if it all went according to plan. At least the human race would be left to live normally again, for which they should all be thankful.

⤴⤵

Using a remote handling device, Professor Milton Rhodes held up the little creature, inspecting it thoroughly. In form, it resembled the first hatchling they'd seen. Genetically, however, it was pure. The flaw had been identified correctly by him and Barbara, and his colleague from the other side of the ocean concurred. Together they'd discovered and examined the satellites — short sequences of DNA used as genetic markers to track inheritance factors — and identified the karyotype of the individual selected for the project. It was a true hybrid — half human and half alien and it looked ghastly. It could not speak, but Brother Emmanuel managed to communicate efficiently with it and translated as they progressed.

Once the hybrid understood what was being done, it cooperated willingly with the team. After extensive gene therapy in their well equipped laboratory, both Professors were convinced they had the solution, and now the first of a batch of fresh eggs had hatched. The little being squirmed and wriggled, but understood instantly that it did not need a host to survive.

Professor Hynes smiled as his colleague placed it back in its artificial environment, sealed off from the rest. They'd succeeded in their initial task, and a bottle of chilled sparkling wine was passed jubilantly around the laboratory.

Outside, up and down the coast, the relatively few remaining adult hybrid aliens stopped whatever they were doing. A telepathic message was being received and it was enough to cause every one of them to respond to the silent call. In droves they moved slowly towards the laboratory where a new little brother was calling. His voice was pure and strong, and the message he was sending was powerful.

⊿↷

Brother Emmanuel smiled. The work he'd done over the past few days had been rewarding — far more so than he'd anticipated. He'd communicated with the entire race — the new, pure Gardaarians — and they'd elected him as their representative on this planet. He learned of their transport lying on the far side of the moon, and their burning desire to make amends.

The discovery that their hosts were actually helping them to survive was a revelation — until now every species their race encountered had aggressively hampered their efforts until they eventually disappeared, diluted to the point of extinction. They were now desperately trying to try to undo what harm they may have caused to this quite different species — the human race.

President Jackson put his hand on the Jesuit's shoulder and flashed his teeth once more for the press. The sun was shining brightly and his features were clearly seen by five billion humans worldwide as he pointed to the medal he'd just pinned on the young man's breast. The Universal Medal for Outstanding Achievement in the Field of Intergalactic Relations was a new award he'd dreamed up for the occasion. The other three already wore theirs.

"This is a great angle, Brother. Pull in the religious vote for sure," the President said quietly through clenched teeth as he widened his toothpaste commercial smile.

Since the last of the pure aliens had been sent off, the whole planet was in celebratory mode. Party time in a big way had arrived, particularly over on the western seaboard where the last alien vegetation was being disposed of. It had even spread inland as far as the desert settlements.

The group smiled once more; Doctor Barbara Westville and Professors Rhodes and Hynes backed Brother Emmanuel and the President as the world's press jostled and shoved for better angles.

"I think that's enough for now, don't you?" the President turned to Barbara and indicated the way back into the building.

"Let's get away from this lot — I need a bit of peace and quiet," he added as they followed.

In the comfort of his office, the four visitors sat sipping coffee as the throng outside slowly dispersed. Ignoring the Professors and the Jesuit Priest and turning to the beautiful blonde sitting across from him, President Rodriguez Jackson flashed his teeth once more.

"Barbara my dear, what really caused those halfbreed creatures to change their minds like that? After all, my Military Advisors were under the impression that their sole aim was to take over the planet, but then they suddenly reversed course, as it were, and committed mass suicide. That is, if what the press out west in crazyland is to be believed. What really happened?"

Barbara straightened up and took a deep breath, her action pushing her straining laced bodice almost to the limit, an action that instantly gained closer scrutiny by the nation's First Citizen.

"Well, Mr. President," she began.

"Call me Rod, please. You too," he added, casting a cursory glance towards the three men at her side.

"Well, as you know," she continued, "the aliens arrived in the form of eggs many millennia ago. Their craft landed on the far side of the moon and the eggs were brought to our planet by a smaller vessel, but somehow it was buried under many layers of lava and then sedimentary rock. They learned of this by communicating with the computer that guided their ship to-"

"Yeah, yeah, I know all this," President Jackson interrupted. "What happened to change their minds is what I'd like to know. Was it the realisation that our Military was about to finish them off? According to General Quigley they knew they'd tangled with the wrong guys this time and we kicked their collective ass. That the way you all see it?"

Barbara studied the First Citizen for a few moments before replying. His cheeks were lined but taut, probably as a result of continually smiling. His greying hair was carefully styled — not a strand was out of place, and his grey eyes flicked continuously from her face to her bustline. She was used to it — his hungry gaze strayed over her body the whole time she was in his presence, which over the last few days had been often. His reputation as an incorrigible ladies' man was evidently well-earned.

"Rod," she began, noting the pleased result of her informality, "the aliens came to our world purely by chance. They'd become almost extinct on their home planet and they had to find a new host species — their galaxy was worked out. They'd used up all the other life-forms there. They had to live in symbiosis with a host initially, but they would modify the genes — mix in with theirs, always trying desperately to find a balance to counteract the inherent flaw in their genetic makeup. Well," she raised her hand as he leaned forward to interrupt, "they found us. They were programmed to do exactly what they did — to find a host as quickly as possible, obtain new genetic material and adapt fast. The botanical worker we found dead was the initial source of their human DNA. They breed so fast that they soon —"

"Yeah, yeah. Barbara, I know all this stuff —"

"Please, Mr President," she noted his disappointment, "let me put this in the correct perspective. They never considered the needs or feelings of any of the host species they used. They were programmed to survive at any cost. So they did just that, without taking into account that we live here too. That's how it was, on every planet they took over. When they were done, there were never any original inhabitants left — they would use up the population and move on when the strain became too diluted — too weak to support their faulty immune systems.

"Now, for the first time, they found a species that could communicate with them. Through Brother Emmanuel here," she gestured towards the fair haired young man sitting next to her, "they found that not only were we able to understand their problem, we could also fix it and give them the ability to survive on their own, for the very first time in their history. They have no idea how or when their problem developed. They may be technologically capable of travelling across the stars, but they never managed to find out what was wrong within themselves."

"So, Barbara, because we could talk to them, we scared them off, is that it?"

Barbara looked at her President with something bordering on disdain. "Not quite, Mr. President. When they realised what we'd achieved, they were stunned. Nowhere in their travels had they ever found a species willing to help them. They'd always encountered hostility and aggression, which is why they were programmed to respond in the manner they did. The concept of an alien nation assisting them was staggering. They'd never imagined anything like it, and they realised immediately that we were their ultimate salvation.

"Accordingly, their mass consciousness, for that's what it is, decided to cleanse the collective being of all extraneous genes and begin again, with our assistance. The 'mass suicide' the press is so fond of describing is how they purged their race of the mixed genetic material. The new, dynamic strain developed fast. And the result is the cargo of genetically pure eggs now on its way to the moon on board one of our shuttles. The construction and technical crews out at Luna Base Two have checked out their ship — it's ready to begin the long voyage back to their home world with an onboard colony of pure Gardaarians."

President Jackson stared at her. "So, in other words, we've won. We kicked their ass and they're on their way home and planet Earth is free of all alien life forms — apart from that pesky vegetation that they're still getting rid of out west. That right?"

"Yes, Mr. President, we've won — I suppose you could call it that. The triumph of the human spirit; helping your neighbour is what won. It's in our nature to help our fellow being, although sometimes I wondered about that, watching your Military Advisors operating over the last few weeks."

There was a long silence while the President absorbed her speech. In the end he bowed his head.

"The population of Earth will be eternally grateful to you people," he said humbly, finally acknowledging the others sitting watching the repartee with faintly amused looks on their faces.

"You've saved countless people from a horrible experience. God knows how many casualties we sustained before —"

"One. Just one, Mr President, and even that one is debatable. We could have done something for Matt Lusted if we'd got to him before the medics at —"

"Matt who?"

"Matt Lusted, the member of the botanic support staff who was the apparent donor of human DNA."

"Yeah, right, him. Still, there would have been many more —"

"We received something perhaps as valuable to our species in return though," she interrupted, watching the President through narrowed eyes.

"They gave us something? What?" President Jackson sat up straighter, staring at the well-built blonde across his desk.

Barbara Westville concentrated her thoughts and focussed on the man sitting in front of her. She could feel the process becoming simpler with each attempt. The endless hours of practise she'd had with the young Jesuit was making it easier each time — she found she could read thoughts with very little effort now. It was time to practise sending them.

"Barbara? What did they give us in return?" he asked again.

"For those of us with sufficient mental competence, the ability to communicate telepathically, Mr President. To be able to read thoughts and convey ideas, sometimes across vast distances, with no mechanical or electronic means. They're advanced telepaths, and their powers have been rubbing off on us since the first eggs hatched." She narrowed her eyes even more, the blue flashes just visible through dark slits now.

And no, there's no way in hell I would ever join you for what you have in mind, bozo! she shot at him, vastly pleased at the way her President jerked upright, his face a caricature of shock and embarrassment.

At her side, Brother Emmanuel smiled to himself. The world would never be quite the same again, that was for sure.

Richard O. C. Cousens

Just the right side of 60, born in Cape Town, South Africa and a long time resident of Durban, where I currently teach English to Chinese pre-university students. Worked successively as a Navigating Officer with the British Royal Fleet Auxiliaries, in gold mines near Johannesburg, as a salesman of, in succession, candy, soft drinks, liquor, solar heating and home security systems. Built a fifty-foot ocean-going yacht in the backyard and sailed to Europe with my wife and three young children. Lived aboard while working on oil rigs in the North Sea and Northern Norway. On the return voyage, the yacht was wrecked on Tristan da Cunha. Semi-retired since 1998, became more serious about my first love — writing. Completed three full-length SF novels, none of which have been published. Surf as often as possible (long board) in the warm waters of the Indian Ocean nearby, hike in the mountains inland from Durban and enjoy life immensely. Appreciate fine wine and good music.

Academic Freedom
Richard Ferris

The blue and white planet rapidly filled the canopy of the Imperial Research Vessel *Relic*, the craft's course taking it on a low velocity decent into the atmosphere. Dr. Wallace Taoshi, sitting at the battered and stained pilot's console, looked up through the canopy and made several adjustments to their entry vector.

"We'll be landing on the continent designated… number one in the northern hemisphere. Take some readings and giving me some potential sites," Dr. Taoshi called into the back of the ship.

"Right, Doc. I am beginning metallurgic, chemical, radiological and life form scans," the chipper voice of Jill Amistad responded.

"Thank you, Jill. You should come up here soon. The view is beautiful. What was the name of this planet again?"

"Doesn't have one Doc. It's designation is XOP3658. It was only recently charted. The scout team said they found the remains of a lot of large structures in numerous locations. Who knows, it may be one of the mythical Lost Worlds."

Dr. Taoshi chuckled, "Wouldn't that make my career! Not to mention your Doctoral research in Outer Rim Xeno-archeology much more interesting."

Jill replied in only mildly sarcastic tones, "Come on Doc, ruined cities paved in gold? Where there are cures for plagues and the fountain of youth exists? Those are children's stories. If they had really existed why would we have left them?"

Jill checked her computer screen and said, "I am getting the first readings now. Scans show a lot of life forms down there, but just flora and fauna. The rest of the readings show a high concentration of, well, everything. Particularly on the eastern coast of the continent in question. It might have been a huge metroplex once from all the metallurgic readings. I'll transmit some landing coordinates in the center of it."

A few moments later he responded, "Thanks Jill. I have the coordinates laid in. Hold on."

"Wait! Let me strap in," Jill yelled as she threw herself into the nearest chair and buckled in. The *Relic* made a sharp forty-five degree right bank into a nosedive. Jill's head slammed against the headrest. A moment later she was thrown against the harness as Doctor Taoshi leveled out of the dive and cut the speed. Relaxing, Jill brushed her auburn hair out of her face.

"Doc! Why do you torment me with your so-called piloting skills? Where did you get your operator's license anyway? A box of Devart Sugar Crackers?" Jill yelled.

"Oh hush. I am a perfectly good pilot and you know it. I just have a sense of adventure. And it was a package of Alterian Candy Snappers, if you must know," Doctor Taoshi replied dryly.

"Doc, please just land this thing… carefully."

"Of course my dear Jill. When haven't I?"

"Well, there was that time on Alteria III when you…."

"Yes, yes, yes. I received poor flight direction from the traffic controller. It wasn't my fault."

"Sure Doc, whatever."

"Remember who is grading your doctoral dissertation young lady," Dr. Taoshi replied with a smile in his voice.

"I can't finish it if I am dead."

"Details, details," Dr. Taoshi shot back as he brought the *Relic* in over a river. "There are the remains of a bridge off to the left. Looks relatively advanced."

Turning her head, Jill looked out the view port and studied the structure. "Looks like it was a draw bridge of some sort. We may want to check it out later," she responded. Jill unbuckled her safety harness and headed up to the cockpit.

Dr. Taoshi looked up at her with his intelligent and mischievous blue eyes. He smiled and motioned for her to sit. Jill took up the co-pilots chair and strapped in again. Dr. Taoshi's landings could be a little rough. With his messy silver hair and slightly wrinkled face, most of his students never guessed what kind of a mad man he was sometimes. Jill had learned in the last two years as his graduate assistant just how wrong that assessment was.

Dr. Taoshi smiled, looked over into her hazel eyes and said, "Hold on." He then took the *Relic* though a barrel roll and landed it in a large open green expanse of land.

⤢⤡

Jill walked down the *Relics* port entry ramp, glad to be on solid ground for the first time in two and a half days. The fresh air of the planet felt rather invigorating. It smelled a little strange, but that was to be expected, every planet had a different smell to it. This smell was the sweet aroma of trees and flowers untouched by any human hand. It made her think back to her youth, on Englara.

She took a few steps out and made her first archeological find on the planet. Half buried in the grass was a coin of some sort, rather battered and beaten. She held it up and looked at it. The coin had the head of a male human figure on one side and a temple of sorts on the other. There was some writing on both sides, but in a language she could not recognize.

Dr. Taoshi stepped off the ramp and looked over her shoulder. "I always said you had the makings of a fine archeologist. Not even on this planet for two minutes and already you've found something."

"Here," Jill said as she tossed the coin to Dr. Taoshi. "Do you know the language, oh great and wise one?"

"Let's see…," he said without missing a beat. "No, I don't recognize it. I will run it though the computer tonight. It should be able to give us some idea."

"Wow, That's the building I want to check out," Jill said as she pointed to a large building to their right. It was a massive structure that dominated the southern end of the area they were in. "Massive columns, it's topped with a large dome. Do you see that statue on the top? It looks like there was an eastern wing to the building, but it's not there anymore. About sixty percent looks to still be standing."

"Offhand, without any investigation, what would your hypothesis be about its function?" Dr. Taoshi asked quietly.

"Given it is sitting on a small rise or hill top in a rather prominent place, I would have to guess it is a temple of some sort. It is too small, not grand enough really, to be a government building."

"Don't let your culture influence your thinking. Just because the Imperial family and the lesser noble families have palaces that take up over four hundred acres does not mean this couldn't be a government structure," the doctor admonished.

"True, but most government buildings are either very grand or very plain and functional. This is… both, in a way."

"So, what would that say about this culture if that were true?"

"That they believe government to be important but, easily accessible? Come on. That sounds like something a Resistance member would say. Only they would say it in more harsh ways."

"Be that as it may. We have the remains of what looks to be a large city to survey. Let's go grab some of the gear and start up with basic protocols. You do remember those, correct?"

"I memorized them in your 101 class, Doc. I didn't sleep though it like other people," Jill responded as she headed back up the ramp of the ship.

⟳⟲

Dr. Taoshi, one of the Imperial Academy's finest archeologists, sat down on the lowest steps of the building that had so intrigued his student. He had spent the better part of the last six standard hours putting surveillance, measurement, and recording equipment into place in what was roughly a two-kilometer area. He looked up at the large structure. He had to admit, she was probably right. All the Imperial government buildings he had ever seen, all the government structures he had ever dug up, on over ten long-term expeditions, all fell into one of two categories. They were either starkly functional or overly grand and ostentatious.

The only exceptions were the remains of very primitive societies that hand no real central government. All of which played into the hands of the Imperial Information Bureau's "proper ideological" teaching guidelines. Well, the nice thing about these first survey missions was that you got out from under the Imperial government and its rules.

Looking at the building his mind kept racing back to all the myths he, and everyone else, had ever heard about the mythical Lost Worlds. Their near perfect government and completely impartial judicial system. Their freedoms from want and hunger. And also about their eventual demise.

Dr. Taoshi looked at the coin Jill had found and spun it between his fingers. He stood up and walked back to the ship. He needed to start running tests on the language. Maybe that could give them some clue about who built all this.

⟨⟩⟩

Jill finished setting up the last of the survey markers when she saw it. Another building, similar but different from the large one she had first seen. She walked to it and started to study the open-air temple like structure from a distance. It must be a temple she thought. She could make out more details the closer she got. There was a fairly tall statue of a man seated in a chair. He was a very authoritative god like figure, yet had a fatherly look to him. He must be the head or near the head of the pantheon of their deities, she concluded.

She started towards it again, but stopped. Jill realized just how late it was getting. She grabbed her comm-link from her belt and activated it. "Doc, I found another temple. This has to be a temple, not a government building. It is getting kind of late, do you want me to check it out or head back?" she asked.

"Why don't you come back to the ship, Jill, I have started cleaning the coin for language analysis."

"That reminds me. I found another coin, this one is made of copper, I think. Different figure on one side but the other side is too dirty and worn to make anything out."

"Bring it back and we can start to clean it up and analyze it with the other one," Dr. Taoshi responded.

"Okay, I am on my way."

When Jill arrived on the ship Dr. Taoshi was already cleaning the coin she had found earlier. He was doing it by hand instead of laser or chemical solution. He could be such a traditionalist sometimes, Jill thought to herself.

"Here is the coin I found," Jill said as she handed the coin over to him. Dr. Taoshi put the first coin on the Language Interpretation Unit, or LIU, and took the offered coin. He examined it closely

"This is in terrible shape, you just had to pick one like this didn't you?"

"You're right, I did it just to annoy you Doc. It was sitting next to a bright and beautiful example of a coin. But I decided to grab this one just to make life difficult," Jill replied, smiling at him.

"Anyway, I will run this one through the chemical wash. It will need it. Then you can finish cleaning it."

An hour later the LIU beeped. Jill and Dr. Taoshi got up from their meager dinner and headed over to the unit. Dr. Taoshi looked at the read-out for a minute. Then a puzzled look crossed his face.

"What's wrong Doc?" Jill asked.

"According to the interpretation unit this is Pre-Expansion English."

"Pre-Expansion English? How could that be? There were no star-faring colonies, this far out, that used that."

"Not entirely true my young student," Dr. Taoshi said with a wink. "There were some very early colonies that may have used it. They would be ancient even by our standards. Of course they are all tied to the mythical Lost Worlds, like Earth."

"Even if that were true, the earliest colonies were well beyond the use of coinage. Mostly using primitive credit chips and such."

"Yes, that's true. Let's see what the coins actually say. That might help us," Dr. Taoshi said as he picked up the larger coin. He grabbed a scanning pad from the LIU and waved it over the obverse side of the coin.

"Interesting. This says, here on the left it says 'IN GOD WE TRUST'. A religious statement, how interesting. On the right, it says 'LIBERTY' with the numerals 2098. 'Liberty.' I wonder what that means. I have never heard the word before, have you?"

"Um, yes, actually," Jill hesitantly replied.

"Really, in what context?"

"Well, the Resistance and the Students for Justice use it. It is defined as freedom with reasonable restrictions."

"Fascinating... freedom with... wait a minute. Jill, how do you know this?"

"I am a college student Dr. Taoshi, I have friends in low

places. And don't look at me like that. Do you think I would jeopardize everything I have, or have the potential to have, for some silly ideology?"

"Point taken, Jill. As it is, there is no way the Imperium will let us bring something like that back. They would confiscate it and it would never see the light of day. We would probably be interrogated for a few days to boot."

"Doc? What if we tell them we could not translate it? Or that the translation made no sense?" Jill said hopefully.

"Lie, for the sake of academic progress? Jill my girl, I see I am having a good influence on you. Now what do you think the numbers mean?"

"It is too large to be a number of religious significance. Those are usually one- or two-digit numbers. I would guess it is the year it was put into circulation."

"That would be my guess as well. Since we don't have any calendar to compare it to the year is irrelevant for the moment," Dr. Taoshi said. "What would your conclusion be about this coin so far?"

"That it was minted as a tribute to a deity. In this case it would be a God of Freedom. I know that is a dangerous way of looking at it."

"I have to agree with your assessment though," Dr. Taoshi said. "Now lets look at the reverse side, shall we." He turned the coin over and ran the scanning pad over it. Jill looked over his shoulder and her eyes went wide as she read.

"Doc, the bottom line on the coin, it says 'UNITED STATES OF AMERICA'. I have never heard of that colony or political entity."

"It is an unfortunate truth that much of our pre- and early space travel history was lost during the First Domination War. For all we know, we could very well be standing on Earth, the home world of the Lost Worlds. You have to remember every myth has some basis in truth."

"If that were true, that would mean Englara is not the original home world of humanity. It would fly in the face of two thousand years of history... or propaganda. This would shake the very foundation of... well... everything. Not the least of which the Imperium and the Imperial family."

"Now Jill, before we go off fomenting revolution let's look at the rest of what we have. Here it says 'FIVE CENTS', no doubt the currency's value. This word here is 'MONTICELLO'. I wonder what that is a reference to?"

"Perhaps it is the name of the God of Freedom, and that building is his main temple? Monticello the God of Freedom. It is strange that they did not put it on the side with his face," she said.

"That is true. However, it is a working hypothesis, for now, anyway. Here is the interesting thing," Dr. Taoshi said as he pointed to the top of the coin, "this is not in any form of English. The unit identified it as Latin, 'E PLURIBUS UNUM'. The translation from that would be 'from one many,' how curious."

"I have never heard of Latin. Is it a human language?"

"There is no information in the database about that."

"What are two different languages doing on the same coin?" Jill asked, looking puzzled.

"Lets have a look at that other coin you found," Dr. Taoshi said as he picked it up. "You did a good job cleaning this one. Now this is interesting. On the obverse side it has a different bust but the same words. In god we trust and liberty. The numerals are different however. This one reads 2010. If these numbers are years then this is quite a bit older that the first."

"The clothing and hair styles on the two figures are quite different." She pointed out as she took the coin. She examined it closely and then noted, "There is a small letter, a 'D', on it. I wonder how significant that is?"

"What is on the other side, Jill?" Dr. Taoshi asked.

Jill turned the coin over and gasped. "That, that is the temple I saw just before I called you. It is not that far from here."

"You didn't notice this when you were cleaning it?"

"I used the chemical solution, ran the laser over it quickly, and put it in the LIU."

"Fair enough. What of the writing?" Dr. Taoshi asked.

"Oh, the same as the other, the Latin inscription with United States of America. However it says 'ONE CENT'. I guess this is a lesser denomination that the first."

"It looks like the coins have given us more questions than answers. Let's sleep on it, shall we. In the morning we can look at that temple you found."

Starting off towards her room she called over, "All right, good night Doc."

"Good night."

Later that night, Jill checked to see if Dr. Taoshi was asleep. He was. She quietly made her way to the cockpit and turned on the communications console. She made a single coded burst transmission on a hyper-wave frequency. She erased her activities from the communications log and shut down the console. She quickly made her way back to her room and went to sleep.

The next morning found Jill in a gray shirt and black slacks with strong hiking boots. She looked around and could not stop admiring how nature had could reclaim so much of what it had lost. You could hardly tell there was a city here at all in some places. If it were not for the ruins and the rather large remains such as the one to the south and the temple she found earlier, there would be no evidence at all.

She sighed and remembered this just made her job, as an archeologist, that much harder. She was considering these things as Dr. Taoshi walked up to here in an awful bright lime green one-piece survival suit and blue boots. Jill stifled a laugh and started to make a comment about his lack of fashion sense, but stopped herself.

"Are you ready doc?" she asked.

"Show me the way, my fearless student," Dr. Taoshi replied with a grand sweeping gesture. After a five-minute walk they found themselves looking at a large temple like structure. The one Jill had seen the day before. Jill stopped and looked around.

"This pond here in front of the temple. It looks like it may be the remains of a man made pool. It is a little too perfect," Jill stated.

"You are right, it could be a reclaimed pool of some sort. Let's keep moving to this temple."

"Right. This way, but watch your step, it is a little rocky."

Within minutes they were at the base of the temple looking up. Jill said, "This is as far as I got last night. Pretty impressive if you ask me."

"Well, take some readings before we go in. It does not look to be in the best of shape. We should be careful."

Pulling out a measure/scan unit, Jill began taking the readings and measurements of the structure. As the structure's statistics started to scroll across the screen she read them off. "Height of building is roughly 30.10 meters give or take for environmental erosion. The colonnade is about 57.30 meters long and 36 meters wide. The columns are 13.41 meters tall. All of it is made of marble. Actually several different types were used."

"That should be enough for now, Jill. Let's take a look at the inside," Dr. Taoshi said as he started up the stairs. Jill quickly shut off the unit and followed.

The two researchers entered the structure only to be amazed at the size of everything. "That statue is at least 6 meters tall. It is in pretty good condition too."

"Jill, come look at this," Dr. Taoshi called from the far wall.

She walked up and looked at the wall and said, "It looks like a proclamation or edict of some sort." Dr. Taoshi turned a scanning pad from the language interpretation unit to the words etched in the marble. "Some of the words are too worn to get an accurate translation, but let's see what we can do. Maybe it will give us some idea of who this was or what he stood for." Dr. Taoshi let the unit run for several minutes to get a good scan of the wording.

Finally he announced, "It's finished. However there are some gaps. But it translates as:

> Four score and seven years ago our fathers brought
> forth on this continent a new nation, conceived in liberty
> and dedicated... all Men are created equal... engaged
> in a great civil war, testing whether that nation or any
> nation so conceived and so dedicated can long
> endure... We have come to dedicate a portion of that
> field as a final resting-place for those who here gave their
> lives that that nation might live. The brave men, living and
> dead who struggled here have consecrated it far above
> our poor power to add or detract... can never forget
> what they did here. It is for us the living rather to be
> dedicated here to the unfinished work ... so nobly
> advanced. It is rather for us to be here dedicated to the
> great task remaining before us — that from these
> honored dead we take increased devotion to that cause

for which they gave the last full measure of devotion —
that we here highly resolve that these dead shall not
have died in vain, that this nation under God shall have a
new birth of freedom, and that government of the
people, by the people, for the people shall not perish
from the Earth.

"Wow," was all that Jill could say. She looked up at the statue
again and back at the wall. She finally looked up at her mentor.
"These are not the words of a god, but of a man. He was not a
god, but a leader, a great leader. I wonder who he was? I suppose that is what we are here to find out. Right Doc?" Dr. Taoshi
did not respond. "Doc, what's wrong?"

"I have spent my entire life devoting myself to the cause of
knowledge. But it was a knowledge always tainted by the strictures of the Imperial Academy's Code of Conduct. I could not
advance any research that could undermine the Imperial family
or the Imperium. I had no academic freedom, I have no liberty,
and I didn't even know the word. Yet here is a leader commemorating those who fought for such… abstract concepts. A leader
thanking his soldiers, when was the last time an Emperor or any
member of the Imperial family was seen thanking soldiers for
their sacrifice?"

"You always said that the knowledge was the important
thing, not ideology."

"I was wrong. I can see that now. It is important. They will
come and destroy everything here. It is too dangerous for them
to let it stand. For these ideas to get out."

"Why?" Jill asked with a strange, almost bemused look on
her face.

"Why what? Why would it be too dangerous? The moment
that the concept of government of the people, by the people
and for the people gets out, people will want it. And if there
were historical examples for such a government, it would make
things even worse. It could start a revolution."

"Would that be so bad? After all wouldn't you like to study
the past with out the Imperial Academy looking over your shoulder? Wouldn't you want justice for everyone, regardless of
whether or not they were human? And maybe it is not achiev-

able, but it is certainly something worth striving for. Isn't it?"

"Jill… I never considered you to be…."

"Anything more than a good student of archeology. Perhaps it is time for a revolution. Everything changes. Look around you; this was probably once a well landscaped park in a huge city with millions of people. Now look at it."

"People die in revolutions, change can be bloody and painful. And who knows what the end result will be?" Dr. Taoshi asked looking straight into Jill's eyes. She didn't flinch.

"Is that Doctor Wallace Taoshi talking, or the Imperial Information Bureau?" she retorted sharply. Dr. Taoshi broke eye contact and stood stunned, unable to reply. Jill quietly turned on her heel and left him standing in front of the statue.

Dr. Taoshi returned to the *Relic* several hours later. The ship was closed, Jill nowhere to be found. He opened the entry ramp and went inside. The lights were on in the cockpit and analysis area, but nowhere else. He sat heavily in the pilot's seat and looked at the controls. It was hard, so hard, to make a decision like this. Jill's attitude didn't help, the idealism of youth.

Suddenly his comm-link beeped. Looked down and turned it on. "Yes. Jill where are you?" he asked quickly.

"Doc, you won't believe this. I found an archive of some sort. There are a lot of items that are completely ruined, but a few survived using rather primitive stasis techniques. You have got to see this." She spoke in the eager student voice he had come to know.

"Where is this place?"

"Set your comm-link to homing frequency one, that should get you here. It is not that far from the ship actually."

"I am on my way."

Jill met Dr. Taoshi at the rubble filled doorway of the building. Her face beamed as she smiled. He could see she had a LIU scanning pad with her. "Come on," she admonished him as he approached. She quickly led him into a rubble-strewn room that stank of stale air. Inside there was broken glass and marble everywhere. Numerous documents were beyond salvage. One document however survived in a primitive stasis field in a very prominent place in the front of the room. As he walked over to it, Jill handed him the LIU scanning pad. He looked at the document on the wall and then at the pad. He slowly read the translation. His first observation was that of an academic.

He said, "The date on the document is over four hundred years before the first coin we found."

She stared at him for a moment and said, "Yes, but read the document."

"I did, remarkable. It is truly remarkable. These people revolted from their king and established a nation, based on liberty and equality that lasted at least four hundred years. You were right Jill, maybe revolution would not be such a bad thing."

"Actually doctor, that kind of talk will get you killed," a deep male voice said behind them. Both of them turned around and looked on in shock as they found themselves looking at three Imperial Enforcement Agents. They stood there in identical outfits, black pants and silver jackets over white shirts. One of them was holding a particle pistol at the doctor.

"What... who... how?" Dr. Taoshi asked rather flustered.

"Don't play innocent with us. We detected a burst transmission to a Resistance cell from these coordinates. Who would of thought the famous Doctor Wallace Taoshi a traitor to the Imperial crown?"

"But I am not! I have no idea what you are talking about. You will seriously regret this error agent," he replied walking toward the agent who was holding the pistol at him.

"Doc," Jill started, "I can explain. It was —"

"Not now Jill."

"But."

"Not now!"

"Take one step closer to me Doctor Taoshi and I will use deadly force," the agent said in a rather bored tone of voice. The doctor took one step closer, the agent fired, a bolt of charged particles hurled into his chest sending him sprawling onto the ground.

The next moment, in one swift motion, Jill's right hand pulled a small blaster from her jacket pocket and unleashed two bolt of energy in the agent who had shot her mentor, dropping the agent. She quickly turned and sent two more bolts into the man on the left and he fell in agonizing pain. She fired her last shot at the agent on the right and missed. He returned fire but missed as Jill dove behind a fallen column.

She could hear the agent walking around towards her. She crouched and got ready to jump at him. A moment she heard the sound of numerous energy bolts fill the room. She saw the agent's dead body drop to the ground in front of her.

Jill slowly looked up over the fallen column she was hiding behind, and breathed a sigh of relief. There, at the doorway, armed with repeating particle rifles where members of her resistance cell. The ones she had contacted the night before.

"Took you guys long enough to get here," Jill spat out.

"Well, we needed to make a dramatic entrance," the tall blonde man holding a rifle replied.

Jill did not respond but ran over to Dr. Taoshi. She looked at him, his eyes started to flutter. "Doc, Doc! Talk to me, Doc!" she cried. She heard the Resistance members run over. One of them pulled her away and began administering first aid.

The medic looked up after a minute. "It does not look good," he reported, "but he is conscious." Jill kneeled next to him, holding back tears with a deep sigh. She was about to apologize, but Dr. Taoshi spoke first.

"Jill, my life was… about…," he coughed, "teaching people what they need to know…about knowledge. This knowledge must get to the people, they all need to know."

"Doc, can you hang in a little longer?"

"After a lifetime… of sitting though faculty meetings… I think I have the willpower to hang on a little longer. Why?"

Jill turned to the tall blonde man. "Jorzan, do we still have the codes to break into the galactic televid network?"

Jorzan looked at her skeptically. "Yes, but we will only be able to break in for a few minutes. After that the codes are useless."

"Fine, this is that important."

"But, Jill —"

"Trust me."

With a sigh Jorzan nodded to two men and they began setting up communications and decryption gear. Jorzan walked over to help. After several minutes, during which Jill kept a close eye on Dr. Taoshi, the gear was set up and the camera was in place.

Jill looked at the man who had been her mentor for the

past two years. A tear slowly made its way down her face. "Doc, just read this, read what we found in here, so everybody will hear these words. Inspire people." Dr. Taoshi nodded and grabbed the LIU pad.

He looked up at the cameraman, who in turn looked to Jorzan who gave a thumbs-up. They were in the galactic televid network.

With a sigh, Dr. Taoshi looked into the camera and began. "My name is Doctor Wallace Taoshi of the Imperial Academy of Archeology. I am... coming to you via a pirate Resistance transmission. I have to make the announcement that I am on the fabled Lost Home World... Earth. On this planet I have discover that humanity truly did have a great amount of wisdom. Listen to the word of one of their statesmen, this is your rightful heritage." He stopped for a moment, collected himself and began. "We hold these truths to be self evident, that all men are created equal; that they are endowed by there creator with certain inalienable rights; that among these are life, liberty and the pursuit of happiness. That to secure these rights," Doctor Taoshi began coughing again, he stopped for a moment and continued, "governments are instituted among men, deriving their just powers from the consent of the governed. That whenever any form of government becomes destructive to these ends, it is the right of the people to alter or abolish it, and to institute... new government, laying...," he never finished, his last breath left him and he lay there on the floor, dead.

"They just cut us off, and they have triangulated our position. We need to get out of here!" Jorzan stated. Jill looked around at everyone and got up. With the help of the cameraman she grabbed the document, still inside its stasis field, from the wall. Carrying it they quickly left the building.

On planets all over the Imperium Doctor Wallace Taoshi's words lit a spark. It was a spark for a long forgotten desire; a desire for freedom, for justice. It was a spark that would begin a civil war. A civil war that ultimately would bring down the Imperial House and establish a new government, of the people, by the people and for the people.

Richard Ferris

Richard Ferris is originally a native of San Diego, California and was a "Navy Brat" growing up. He graduated from San Diego State University with a BA in Political Science, despite the best efforts of his high school English teachers to convince him otherwise. He currently resides in St. Paul, Minnesota, with his wife Christina.

The seed for this story comes from an experience in college. An anthropology professor in his Junior year asked: "What would an alien archeologist think of our society thousands of years from now, based on what they found from 1995?" The story was set in Washington, D.C., due to the author's familiarity with it, having lived there for nearly ten years.

This is his second published story. His first, "The Follower," was published in a previous CrossTime Science Fiction Anthology.

໕໒

Finding Magic
F. I. Goldhaber

Ilyana leaned against the door of her chamber. A sharp rapping reverberated in her ear and down her spine. She jumped, and her heart beat faster. When she cracked the door, First Apprentice Shtarn tried to push his way into the cell. Ilyana wedged the toe of her boot under the rough-hewn pine panel before he could force the door more than a hand wide.

"I believe I finally understand why you sought a wizard's apprenticeship, Ilyana," he scoffed, one side of his mouth curling upward. He might be considered handsome by some, with unruly black curls framing a broad brow and strong chin. But as Shtarn looked down at Ilyana, his lecherous gaze made her stomach churn.

"You're not foolish enough to believe a woman could be a sorcerer. This ruse must be your method of finding your way into one of the wizards' beds." He lifted his eyebrows. "You've been at Meech for twelve moons now, and apparently none of them has accepted your offer." Shtarn reached through the opening and lifted her chin with his hand, forcing Ilyana to confront the predatory look in his dark eyes.

"Mayhap you believed your tilted blue eyes and long black hair were enough to entice them, but truth be told you're too skinny and pale for most men to find appealing." Shtarn's gaze ran the length of Ilyana's figure. Fear gave her strength to keep her foot wedged under the door and prevent him from pushing it open though he outweighed her by at least five stone.

"However, I'm not most men and I've decided that you may come to my bed." Shtarn's voice deepened and Ilyana tasted bile. "I realize I'm not yet a wizard, but then you don't have much to offer a wizard. If you prove to be better in bed than you are at Magic, I may keep you around after I receive my journey worker's belt." His hand drifted down Ilyana's neck and came to rest on her breast.

Keeping shoulder and foot against the door, Ilyana grabbed his thumb and removed his hand, almost twice the size of hers. "You are mistaken, Shtarn." She held her chin high and kept her voice defiant. "I do intend to become a wizard and so will never take to any man's bed — wizard or apprentice. Master Glaud has warned me that a sorcerer who loves a man will lose her Power."

Shtarn's jaw dropped and his eyes widened. His distraction allowed her to push the door closed and throw the bolt. Ilyana didn't know if her rejection or the requirement that she remain celibate caused the alteration — males who chose wizardry suffered no such restrictions.

"You will regret turning me away, Ilyana!" Shtarn shouted, banging on the door with a force that shook the three wooden walls separating her cell from those on either side and the corridor. The candle in the sconce beside the door wobbled and sputtered. "I have been kind to you until now. Should you persist in rejecting me, that will end." He pounded on the door again, but Ilyana said nothing. At last, she sensed him returning down the stairs to his own chamber on the level below.

Ilyana sat on her cot and began to weep, her shoulders heaving. The movement loosed her hair from what was left of its braid and it tumbled like a cloak around her shoulders. Ilyana covered her face with her hands. Until incapacitated by illness, Ilyana's father had combed and braided her waist-length hair each morn. Now he was gone and Ilyana wept alone at the top of the wizards' tower, leagues from her home in Leer.

What would become of her? Ilyana had given the wizards almost everything she had inherited from her father to pay for her training. She hadn't enough left, by half, to purchase even the least expensive apprenticeship. Yet, she had learned nothing of value in her twelve moons at Meech. She should have listened to her uncles. They had warned her no good could come of a wizards' apprenticeship. Like Ilyana's father, her mother's brothers were convinced the Magic no longer existed in Lowor.

They feared the Meechian wizards and tried to dissuade Ilyana from believing her grandmother's teachings. Because she persisted in her ambition, both uncles had instructed her not to visit their homes again.

She could have stayed in Leer and purchased a Healers' apprenticeship. The Guild Master had said she'd an aptitude for herbal lore and a healer's touch. Ilyana sighed. Nothing she learned from the Guild during her father's long illness assuaged the overpowering desire that consumed her. And no healer could save her father's life. Despite his age — he had seen but six and thirty summers — Shoril had wasted away before her eyes. At first, only his leg troubled him and it only hurt some of the time. But Ilyana had sensed that what ate away at his bones would destroy him. She had tried to explain the seriousness of his affliction to the healers and begged them to cut off his leg. They only chided her for audacity — a girl of sixteen springs telling journey workers how to ply their trade.

Ilyana had been unable to explain how she knew that whatever was destroying Shoril's leg would feed on his organs as voraciously as a mountain lion devours a deer. All her life, she had been tormented by a second sight. She saw and heard what others did not and at times knew of things before they occurred. When she touched those who were ill or injured, she could sense the source of their pain. Ilyana had learned, when just a child, that if she told others what she learned with her second sight, they thought her possessed and none believed her.

When Shoril's pain became constant and he could no longer walk, the healers pretended not to remember Ilyana's pleas to remove his limb. By then, he was dying and her anger couldn't aid him. Rather than watch him suffer, Ilyana had fed her father tincture of laudanum several times each day for the last three moons of his life.

Since his death, Ilyana had tried to suppress her second sight. Even so, when it assured her that she would find the Magic at the Meechian tower, she had left her home and spent her inheritance for that promise. But, she found no succor here for her burning need to learn. Books were scattered about the wizards' homes, but she wasn't allowed to touch them. Ilyana didn't even know if their pages contained the same runes that her Grandmother Losa had taught her to read and pronounce. The wizards refused to train Ilyana in the ways of the Power. They allowed her to attend lessons in illusion and sleight-of-hand with the other apprentices, but no one would speak to her in the language of the runes and no one would teach her the Magic.

Now Shtarn, either unaware of Master Glaud's admonishment or caring not about it, threatened to make matters worse. Even if celibacy wasn't required, Shtarn's bed offered no appeal. He frightened her almost as much as the wizards did and Ilyana avoided being near him — when she could.

Ilyana pulled off her boot and rubbed the bruise on top of her foot. How would Shtarn punish her resistance? As First Apprentice, he assigned chambers and determined responsibilities. Ilyana already had the least desirable cell in the tower. The wedge-shaped chamber was barely large enough for her cot and was the only one that had no window. A white stone fireplace made up the entire curved outer wall. Although drafty in the winter, Ilyana had been refused permission to bring up wood or coal for a fire. Now, in the stifling heat of summer, she was denied any relief a breeze might bring.

Shtarn could, Ilyana supposed, assign her to serve someone other than Wizard Durn. The old man might be drunk half the time, but he was the only one of the five wizards who had never abused her in some way. When she began her apprenticeship, Ilyana had been assigned to Wizard Borosk. The oldest of the wizards, Borosk's constant pinching left bruises across her backside and breasts. Once he had whipped Ilyana with his belt when she had tripped and broken a flagon of wine.

Ilyana didn't understand why Meechian males acted as if she should be available for a dalliance with any that asked. Until she left Leer, all the men Ilyana knew had been kind to her — her father, her uncles, her cousins, guilders, and other merchants. They had treated her, and as far as she could see all women, with respect. She had always felt safe among them. Was it because these men lived in a large borough? Or mayhap Leer was unique in how its men behaved. Ilyana missed her home.

Tears flowed anew as Ilyana wept for her father, for Losa who had died five summers past, and for the mother she had never known. She wept in despair of ever easing her insatiable hunger to learn the Magic. And she wept in fear of the second sight that haunted and isolated her.

When her sobbing gave way to weariness, Ilyana lay across the thick pile of bedding, her arm under her head. During the winter, she had collected every quilt and comforter she could drag up to her cell to ward off the cold. Ilyana was reluctant to part with them now, even in the suffocating summer heat. Sleeping on top of them was more comfortable than laying across the thin straw mattress of the cot. And they would be needed again in a few moons when the winter winds swept down off the Czelgian Mountains, through the fireplace chimney, and into her cell — if she was still here.

⟁⟂

Sensing rather than hearing the morn's bustle, Ilyana jumped from her cot. Hands on her face, she could feel puffy eyes and a swollen nose. She must look frightful. Mayhap Shtarn and the others would think her ill — Ilyana would prefer they not know she had cried herself to sleep. She pulled a wooden comb through her hair until most of the tangles were gone, then attempted to weave the strands into a braid. It probably would come undone before the day was half over. If not for her father's memory, she would have cut it all off moons ago.

Ilyana smoothed the wrinkles from her cream-colored linen robe as best she could with her hands. The required apprentice garb had been costly. With all she had spent to win a place here, she couldn't afford to purchase a second. She shouldn't have slept in it. Ilyana straightened the sash and the small knife that hung from it in a leather sheath. She cracked her door a whit, peeking out into the corridor. Relieved to see it empty, she ran down the stairs that wound along the inside of the round tower's outer wall.

Two levels below, Ilyana stopped when she saw that servers were clearing away the remains of the apprentices' first meal from the oval table that almost filled the banquet hall. She had slept through her opportunity to break fast with them. At a slower pace, Ilyana continued downward one more length of stairs. The audience chamber was filling with citizens, many with swords at their hips. Heavy tapestries covered the mosaic tiles on the walls and muted the daylight streaming in through the four arched windows above Ilyana's head.

Working around the edges of the throng, Ilyana made her way outside through the arched entrance and around the tower to the privy. Although not that long past dawn, the sun already warmed the air. Ilyana knew to expect a sultry day — warm even by Meechian standards and much hotter than she had ever known in Leer. Breathing through her mouth to avoid the stench of the privy, she stayed no longer than necessary. She dreaded the prospect of spending the entire morn in this heat, crowded on the tower steps with the eleven other apprentices. None of the men bathed regularly and Shtarn wasn't the only one who groped her at every opportunity.

While Ilyana struggled to get water from the well, one of the soldiers guarding the tower came over to offer aid. "Let me get that for you, Apprentice." A strong, heavyset man, Keert had no trouble raising the full wooden bucket and setting it on the stone edge of the well.

"Many thanks, Keert."

The soldier smiled and nodded, then returned to his post. Keert was the only tower guard who did not leer at Ilyana or make lewd comments. Although exchanges between them were brief, his words were always kind. During the winter, when Keert had developed a persistent cough, Ilyana had trudged through the snow in the forest that stood between the tower and the edge of the Czelgian Mountains to find a slippery elm tree. With her knife she had chipped off enough of the bark to make him a decoction. His cough vanished and the soldier now sought opportunities to aid her.

After drinking her fill from the bucket, Ilyana splashed cold water on her face and returned to the tower. She reached the stairs just as a barrage from the clarion players announced the wizards' arrival. All conversation ceased and everyone turned to face the five gilded chairs on the slate dais. The wizards, led by Master Glaud, marched across the chamber, surrounded by soldiers who wore chain mail and carried halberds and swords. Ilyana had been in Meech many moons until she became accustomed to the number of those who came to the tower — soldiers and citizens alike — bearing weaponry and wearing armor. In the small village of Leer, she knew of no one who owned a halberd or even a sword. Knives were used as tools and bows and arrows for hunting game and to show off one's skill in market-day contests.

Wizards Durn, Teester, Kaer, and Borosk followed Master Glaud to the dais. They wore floor-length, cream-colored linen robes decorated at wrists, collars, and hems in crude rune patterns of scarlet, blue, and green. The same colors and patterns adorned the thick, leather belts fastened with copper journey workers' buckles. Golden circlets rested on their heads. Master Wizard Glaud — a short, flabby man starting to lose the brown hair from the top of his head — wore a gold belt buckle and his circlet was set with diamonds. He also wore several gemstone pendants and amulets. Once he settled himself in the largest chair, raised above those on either side, the others took their seats.

The first citizen to approach the dais was a frail woman with an emaciated child in her arms. Falling to both knees and bowing her head to the slate floor, she spoke in a quavering voice that brought a tear to Ilyana's eye. "Oh, noble and mighty Wizards of Lowor, I humbly beseech you to hear my plea."

When Glaud waved a hand for her to continue, the woman lifted her child and crawled closer to the wizards. One of the soldiers who stood at either end of the dais aimed the point of his pike at the woman and she scooted back a little.

"I have been ill for several fortnights and now my child has taken sick as well. I beg you great and merciful Wizards, please help my son."

Why did the woman not seek a healer's aid? The wizards' asked no questions. How could they help, knowing nothing of what ailed her and the child? Ilyana watched Wizard Teester hand the woman a stoppered jar. Wizard Durn said some words Ilyana had never learned and waved his hand over the boy. The woman, clasping the bottle and her son against her chest, stepped to a table at one side of the dais and dropped a handful of silver coins into an ornate casket.

The woman was followed by others who petitioned the wizards for permission to conduct business in the borough or begged them to heal a festering wound or remove pestilence from a herd of cattle. To Ilyana's thinking, too many of the requests seemed more deserving of a healer's attention than a wizard's. And after twelve moons she still didn't understand how the wizards used the Magic to render aid. They would hand out potions, repeat strange words, and at times perform some of the same illusions that Ilyana was studying with Wizard Teester. Ilyana never witnessed anything that resembled her expectations, from Grandmother Losa's tales, of the Magic. Yet all petitioners dropped coins in the casket.

As the morn dragged on, the heat of the day and the bodies surrounding her, the stench of the other apprentices, and her empty stomach caused Ilyana's head to spin. Sweat trickled down between her breasts. Her neck and back were damp under her hair. Leaning her face against the cool, smooth stone of the wall she was able to keep from fainting until Master Glaud at last rose from his chair. Ilyana followed the wizards and the other apprentices up the stairs, finding an empty chair and sitting down before her knees gave way. Apprentices filled their bowls from the pot of stew that stood near their end of the table. Scents of roasted meat wafted over from the wizard's plates on the opposite end. Normally that didn't trouble her, but this day Ilyana's stomach rumbled and she felt weak. She waited until all the men had served themselves, nibbling on the ration of bread she found by her place.

When the other apprentices all were eating, Ilyana stretched toward the pot, but it was beyond her grasp. She walked around the table with her bowl. Without looking at her, Shtarn grabbed the pot. He refilled his half empty bowl and handed the pot to Poeter. Ilyana returned to her seat, but the pot wasn't passed to her. When it reached Lonor, the short stocky apprentice added to his bowl, lifted the pot, and put it in front of Ilyana. She took what was left, but that didn't fill her bowl halfway. Blinking to prevent tears from filling her eyes, Ilyana ate every morsel. She used the rest of her bread to wipe the bowl.

Ilyana didn't know why the other apprentices — with the exception of Poeter, who usually ignored her, and Lonor, who occasionally showed her kindness — tormented her. Master Glaud had warned her that a wizard's studies were long and difficult. Unlike every other guild in Lowor, most wizards' apprentices didn't earn their journey workers' belts. Only five wizards served Lowor and all of them dwelled near the tower at Meech. When one of the five men died, apprentices were judged against one another to determine who would take his place.

Many generations ago, Grandmother Losa had informed Ilyana, wizards served in all four of Lowor's towers. Women were wizards then. The tales Losa had told — how the wizards helped people the healers couldn't aid; protected the boroughs from plague and other epidemics; transformed themselves into different creatures — had fed Ilyana's hunger to learn the Magic. Ilyana longed to earn the right to wear a journey worker's belt and the rune patterns on the edges of her robe. But the other apprentices, convinced a woman could never be a wizard, treated her as if she were at the tower for their amusement. No other guild in Lowor denied women the same opportunities offered men. Why did she have to choose the only one that did?

The wizards had finished their meal and were leaving the banquet hall. Ilyana scurried to take her place with Lonor behind Wizard Durn. The two apprentices followed the Wizard down the stairs. When they walked under the gargoyle guarding the entrance, the midday heat assailed Ilyana. She found herself gasping for breath as she ran to stay with Wizard Durn. Lonor, short as he was compared to other men, had no trouble keeping pace.

When they entered the Wizard's home and Durn flopped down across a plush cushioned bench in his sitting chamber, Ilyana realized he was well into his cups. Durn had seen more than fifty summers. His scraggly silver beard did nothing to disguise his pointed chin and his pale blue eyes gave glimpses of a sad spirit.

"Ilyana, fetch me a cask of mead." Although his voice was nonchalant, Ilyana knew he sought an excuse to be rid of her. While she struggled up the stairs from the tower cellar with a heavy cask on her shoulder, Lonor could learn what the Wizard wouldn't teach Ilyana. Any protest would waste breath, so she turned to leave the house. Again Ilyana tried to keep tears from spilling. She had thought, more than once, about standing outside and using her second sight to "listen" to Lonor's lessons. But she feared being caught either by a soldier asking what she was about or Wizard Durn becoming aware of her intrusion.

With slow steps, Ilyana walked back to the tower. If she hurried, Wizard Durn would find more reasons to send her away so he could work alone with Lonor.

Descending the stairs to the dark cellar beneath the tower, Ilyana stood for a moment enjoying the cool dampness. Her pleasure was chased away by a moan from one of the prisoners. How could she have thought to learn anything good from wizards who used torture and imprisonment to punish citizens? Never privy to the specifics of crimes committed, Ilyana tried not to listen to rumors that reached her ears. She couldn't believe Master Glaud would order a young man tortured to death because the lad was beloved by a woman the Wizard had chosen for his paramour.

Ilyana had never ventured into the dungeon alone before. In the light of the torches flickering along the clammy walls, she could see the row of brick prison cells filling two-thirds of the space. In front of these, where the stairs ended, chains hung from rings in the walls. A tall metal basket of irons stood next to a coal brazier and whips were scattered about the floor. A wood and metal contraption was pushed up against the curve of the wall. Ilyana tried to avoid the notice of those who guarded the prisoners as she made her way along the wall toward the storage area behind the cells.

One of the soldiers spotted her and called out. "Well, Apprentice, have the wizards finally sent you down here to see to *our* needs?" He made sloppy kissing sounds.

Ilyana tried to walk as if she hadn't heard.

"Nay, she's come down because she wants to know what it's like to bed a real man." Out of the corner of her eye, Ilyana could see the rude gesture the second soldier made with a hand near his groin.

As much as she preferred her own company to that of the other apprentices, Ilyana now wished one of them accompanied her. When she was out of the soldiers' sight, Ilyana clutched her stomach, trying not to retch. Someone called her name and she feared one of the guards had followed her. Ilyana turned and looked up, fighting the nausea threatening to remove what little she had eaten from her stomach.

Ilyana could see no one. The only sound she heard was the

whimpering of a man or woman, she couldn't tell which, from one of the cells. She leaned against the wall, gathering courage to return past the guards. Ilyana sensed the Power penetrating the stone from within. Something, not someone, was calling to her from inside the wall.

For a moment, Ilyana wondered if she should ignore the summons. Could anything good be hidden away in the wizards' cellar? Still, what called her wasn't tainted by prisoners' blood. Although she knew of no one else afflicted with a second sight, with one exception hers had always shown her the truth. Ilyana grabbed the first cask of mead she could find and balanced it on her shoulder. Finding strength in the hope that something magical might be hidden in the wall, she carried the cask up the stairs, ignoring the raucous taunts of the soldiers.

She returned with her burden to the splendor of Wizard Durn's home — stark contrast to the misery in the dungeon. The least opulent of the five wizards' dwellings, it had luxuries beyond anything Ilyana had ever known. Instead of dirt covered by rushes, the floor was laid with polished wooden boards. Soft rugs were scattered about and bright tapestries hung from the walls. The moment Ilyana set down the cask, Wizard Durn gave Lonor an affectionate smile and dismissed them both to join the other apprentices at their lessons.

Ilyana's mind turned from the question of what Lonor had learned while she was gone to what could have called to her in the cellar. She found it difficult to give any attention to Wizard Teester's instructions. Never before had she sensed such Power — not even from the wizards when they offered the Magic to the citizens. At times, if Ilyana was unfortunate enough to be standing near Master Glaud, she could sense some Power radiating from him. But on other occasions she was quite close to him and felt nothing at all.

At supper, Lonor sat next to Ilyana and ladled soup into her bowl after his own was full. Although grateful for his thoughtfulness, she didn't taste what she put in her mouth. She must learn more about what was hidden behind the wall in the cellar, no matter the risk. When the wizards left, Ilyana returned to her cell. She stood with her back to the door, listening until all was quiet in the tower.

Ilyana reached out with her second sight to be sure the other apprentices slept and then crept through the corridor to the stairs. No torches burned in the sconces along the curved wall. With the aid of her second sight, and her hand against the stones, Ilyana found her way in the pitch blackness.

When she stood at the bottom of the stairs to the dungeon, pressed against the wall at the edge of the torchlight, Ilyana saw only Keert was on duty. The big man sat with his chair leaning back against the wall, his feet propped up on a small table. An ale flagon rested on its side near the back legs of his chair. Ilyana heard a loud snore, but Keert didn't move.

Creeping around the cells to the back of the dungeon, Ilyana found the spot where she had heard her name called. Sitting on her heels, she brushed her hands against the stones. Something within yearned for her touch. As her fingers explored — her senses open to the stones and what they hid — Ilyana realized this wasn't a true wall. Someone had stacked stones waist high along the southern curve of the tower. Why?

In the dim torchlight that seeped around the edge of the prison cells, careful to avoid scraping stone against stone, Ilyana pulled away pieces of the false wall. After a dozen stones were displaced from where the yearning was strongest, she could reach inside. Her hands touched a thick bundle, wrapped in oiled cloth. She dislodged it from its hiding place.

Although she could sense Power inside the package, Ilyana resisted the urge to open it and learn what had called to her. Instead, she set it down on the packed dirt of the cellar floor and replaced the stones. Her heart pounding against her ribs, she lifted the heavy parcel. Almost half as tall as she, it weighed more than a stone. Holding it close to her chest, she struggled back up the stairs to her cell.

Once inside with the door bolted, she set the package down and wiped the sweat from her forehead with her sleeve. In the darkness of her cell, Ilyana waited until she stopped panting then groped her way to the candle. She brought it near the fireplace and felt about, pulling pieces from the little pile of tinder she had collected. With her flint in one hand and her belt knife in the other, Ilyana struck them together until a spark fired the tinder and she could light the candlewick. Extinguishing the tinder, she tilted the candle over the floor. When enough wax had dripped onto the stone, she secured the candle. She sat cross-legged on the floor, her back to the wooden partition, the wrapped bundle in front of her, leaning against the cot.

With trembling fingers, she pulled away the oiled cloth revealing a tooled, red leather surface. Ilyana's breath caught in her throat. *Shtirm* and *Tslanastan* were carved into the smooth grain of the leather, the same two runes that edged the wizards' robes — only much more elegantly drawn. The leather bound together a stack of parchment pages as thick as both her arms together. Running her fingers over the indentions, the sensation of Power stunned Ilyana. She opened the pages near the middle and saw that the runes Losa had taught her to read covered the parchment.

From the time she could walk, Ilyana spent a part of every day by the riverbank with her grandmother, no matter the weather. Using a stick to draw in the sand, Losa would show Ilyana the shapes of the runes and teach her their meanings and how to pronounce them. Ilyana had been warned not to tell her father of these lessons. Although she didn't understand why, he hadn't wanted her to know how to read. She also learned not to ask Losa questions. Her grandmother wanted Ilyana to know certain things and nothing more. Consumed since she could remember by a need to learn the Magic, Ilyana was grateful to study whatever Losa was willing to teach.

Now, for the first time since Losa had died, Ilyana read the patterns of the runes. "To close a wound that is bleeding," she translated the words on one of the pages, "hold your hand over the injury, pull the Power through the stone, and say: '*Shtirm Tslanastan. Beknort kakera tozlad.*' Draw the rune for healing across the flesh."

Ilyana's eyes filled with tears. Her shoulders shook. The volume contained the Magic that the wizards refused to teach her. Never again would she doubt her second sight — she *would* learn to be a wizard. Turning the pages, she made out spells that could be used to repair a broken bone or to draw venom from someone who had consumed poison. She found spells of protection, spells of joining, and spells of movement. One spell allowed a wizard to take the shape of an animal. Each spell was accompanied by the instructions on how to invoke it as well as a description of its purpose.

Ilyana read until she heard the commotion of the morn outside her door. She hadn't finished a fifth of the volume's pages. Wrapping it back up in the protective oiled cloth, Ilyana buried the volume in the piles of bedding on the cot. She extinguished her candle and joined the other apprentices.

Throughout the day, Ilyana chafed with impatience. She worried that one of the wizards might sense the volume's Power in her chamber and take it from her. Would she be punished for reading it? But the book had called out to *her*. Other apprentices, and sometimes even a wizard, went into the cellar alone. Surely if this book was meant to be read by another, he would have removed it before now?

When Wizard Durn sent her to the kitchen to speak with the cook about supper, Ilyana managed to pilfer extra candles and hide them in the leather purse that hung from her belt. Before she and Lonor left for Wizard Teester's lessons, she filched a small holder from a shelf in the corner and secreted it in her sleeve.

Ilyana begged Wizard Teester to release her from lessons because she was ill. Her claim wasn't hard to believe — she caught a glimpse of her reflection in one of the polished metal mirrors the Wizard used for some of his illusions. Dark shadows rimmed Ilyana's eyes and not even a hint of color touched the skin covering her rounded cheeks.

Tired as she was, Ilyana couldn't bear the thought of closing her eyes without reading more of the parchment pages. She longed to try invoking a spell, but was confused by the instruction to "pull the Power through the stone." What stone did the volume mean — the stone of the tower? Sitting cross-legged on her cot, Ilyana read until she could no longer keep her eyes open. She blew out the candle and fell asleep with one arm wrapped around the volume. At least now she understood what stone was needed to "pull the Power through."

The next morn, Ilyana again missed breaking her fast. She rose so late she hadn't time to get outside to the privy before the wizards entered the audience chamber. Ilyana spent the morn dancing from one foot to the other as the pain in her bladder competed with the wretchedness caused by the heat, her empty stomach, and her exhaustion. Lonor and Shtarn gave her strange looks when she joined the apprentices for dinner after visiting the privy. Ilyana could see Master Glaud glowering at her. For once, his disapproval didn't trouble her. She wanted only for the day to end so she could return to what was hidden in her chamber. After supper, as she headed for the stairs leading to her cell, Shtarn stopped Ilyana with a hand on her arm.

"Which Wizard, Ilyana?" scorn and disappointment colored his voice. Ilyana didn't understand the reason for his insolent sneer and just stared at him. "Which Wizard has taken you to his bed?" When she still didn't answer, Shtarn continued. "You have the look of a woman who has discovered passion for the first time — your eyes are glowing — and you don't appear to have slept well these past two nights."

Ilyana smiled and pressed her fingernails into her palm to keep from giggling. She kept her voice quiet so that only he would hear. "I have found a more appealing companion to bed than you, First Apprentice Shtarn." Leaving him slack-jawed, she pulled away from him and continued up to her cell. Let Shtarn think she was spending her nights in a wizard's bed. She doubted he would vie with one of them for her affections.

In the quiet of her cell, the candle flickered with her breath. Ilyana put her hands on the cover of the volume and opened her second sight to the stone described at the very beginning. To invoke the Magic, a wizard pulled the Power through a ruby. She let the image of this jewel fill her mind's eye and then reached out. The gem, set in a gold ring, was near. She could "see" it lodged between two white stones, covered with dirt. Stepping back in her mind from the image, Ilyana thought the two stones might be on the south side of the tower, opposite the entrance.

How was she to retrieve it without anyone seeing her? During the day, soldiers, wizards, apprentices, servers, and petitioners might be encountered anywhere. Soldiers prowled about the tower throughout the night. If anyone saw her find the ring, she wouldn't be allowed to keep it.

Ilyana decided to attempt one of the spells without a stone to "pull the Power through." She would try something simple. Blowing out the candle, she balanced its holder on the leather of the volume. *"Shtirm Tslanastan. Yichnor queeg fygatein."* She drew the rune for fire over the wick with her finger. Nothing happened. Disappointed, Ilyana used knife, flint, and tinder to relight the candle. She flipped through the parchment pages. Taking a handful of coins from her purse, she closed the volume and scattered the gold pieces across the leather binding. *"Shtirm Tslanastan. Lacharan tshnochnor grasnik."* She traced the rune for movement in the air. The coins remained still. Resting her head in her hands, Ilyana strengthened her resolve. If she must find the ruby to make the Magic work, she would.

The next night, Ilyana waited only until those who lived in the tower were in their beds and then crept back down the stairs. She stopped in the banquet hall and, standing on the table, removed one of the oil lamps that hung by chains from hooks in the stone ceiling. She shut the door to the chamber and made sure both casements and shutters were closed to prevent anyone from seeing a spark or hearing flint strike steel. Covering the flame with a ceramic mug from a shelf next to the massive stone fireplace, Ilyana continued down the stairs. The door that sealed the tower from the outside pulled open easily, despite its weight. She was able to close it again without making a sound.

The moon was almost half full and Ilyana couldn't see anyone about as she crept around to the far side of the tower. Only when the tall white structure stood between her and the wizards' homes did she uncover her lamp. The moon ducked behind a cloud and an owl hooted in the forest behind her causing Ilyana to jump. Calming herself, she knelt in the dirt next to the tower wall and began to search. All the stones looked alike and she couldn't determine which two she had seen in her mind, hiding the ring. With her fingers and her eyes she searched in vain.

She heard the footsteps of the guards as the watch changed and she pressed against the stones, trembling. When the sounds ceased, Ilyana discovered she had been holding her breath and tried to avoid gasping as she pulled air into her lungs. Ilyana lifted the lamp closer to the tower, but still couldn't find the ring. In the forest she heard the rustling of creatures scurrying through the night. A yelp of pain was followed by the triumphant snarl of a wild cat that had captured its prey. Would a hungry cat venture out of the forest to attack a small woman?

The sun would be rising soon and she was beginning to despair. Ilyana decided she was using the wrong senses to seek the ruby. She pictured the ring in her mind, reaching out with her second sight. Her hand wandered of its own accord along the stones, and her fingers probed below the ground in front of the tower. Dirt jammed under her nails and the stones scraped her knuckles, but she felt a bit of metal against one finger. The ring, nestled in a hidden cavity, was buried in the ground.

The dim light of dawn was beginning to creep along the horizon. Ilyana extricated the ring and slipped it, still covered in soil, into the purse on her belt. Rising, she brushed the dirt from her hands and her robe. She extinguished the lamp and walked into the trees. Digging a pit in the dew-dampened pine needles, she buried the lamp and the mug in the roots of a large spruce. Then she made her way around to the privy, hoping if anyone saw her they would assume she had just risen early for once.

Caught up in the morn's activities, Ilyana had no opportunity to examine her treasure. Too elated to eat, she found her hand kept patting the outside of her purse for assurance the ring was still inside. Did she sense a tingle of Power when she did so, or was it just her own excitement? The night's exertions began to take their toll. Ilyana almost fell asleep during Wizard Teester's lessons and had to endure both the Wizard's scolding and the jeering of her fellow apprentices. By supper, knots in her stomach kept Ilyana from eating whatever she ladled into her bowl. Knowing she would regret missing another meal later, she slipped the bread ration into her sleeve and headed for the stairs as soon as she could do so without drawing attention.

Standing in the darkness of the tiny cell, Ilyana leaned against the door. What if she had found just a rock on a ring someone had lost long ago? Even if she could draw Power through this stone — would the wizards be able to sense her use of the Magic and take the ring from her? But Ilyana had removed the volume from the cellar four nights past, wouldn't they have known about it by now? The wizards never came above the second level in the tower, mayhap her cell was too far away for them to sense the Power hidden here. She wasn't conscious of when they used the Magic, even when she stood just across the audience chamber.

Hands shaking, Ilyana dug the volume out of the bedding. She fumbled about until she was sure the candle was steady on the floor. Reaching into her purse, Ilyana touched the ring for the first time since she had pulled it from the dirt and slipped it onto the middle finger of her left hand. The Power in the stone coursed through her body. For several moments she sat in the dark, relishing its strength. She used one corner of a quilt to wipe away the dirt she knew was there but couldn't see.

Touching the candlewick, Ilyana drew the rune for *fygatein*. "*Shtirm Tslanastan. Yichnor queeg fygatein.*" A tiny flame flickered and then the candle was lit. Tears streamed down Ilyana's face and she put her right hand over her mouth to prevent sobs from escaping. She held out her left hand and turned it next to the candle. A huge, tear-shaped ruby, surrounded by nineteen tiny diamonds, sparkled in the light.

Still not believing she had invoked the Magic, Ilyana dropped some coins onto the stones. "*Shtirm Tslanastan. Lacharan tshnochnor grasnik.*" She traced the rune for *lacharan* and the coins began to dance in the air. Ilyana giggled then clamped her hand over her mouth again. But, she hadn't traveled leagues from her home, accepted banishment by her family, and spent most of her inheritance to light candles and play with coins. She thumbed through the parchment pages. When she found the spell she wanted, Ilyana read the words over and over in her mind until she was sure she could recite them without pause. Closing the volume, she pulled her knife from its sheath and pushed the skirt of her robe above her knee.

Hesitating for only a heartbeat, she drew the sharp blade across her shin and gasped as blood trickled over her skin. Dropping the knife, Ilyana put her hand on top of the wound. "*Shtirm Tslanastan. Beknort kakera tozlad.*" With one finger, she drew the rune for *tozlad* in her blood. Her eyes grew wide as the ruby glowed and the cut closed. The bleeding stopped and Ilyana no longer felt any pain. Only a tiny white scar and a red stain of blood betrayed where she had slit her shin.

Exhilarated, but exhausted, Ilyana extinguished the candle and stretched out on her cot. All doubts about her decision to travel to Meech and purchase a wizard's apprenticeship had vanished. She would learn the Magic and fill the empty hole within her spirit — despite the refusal of anyone at the tower to teach her.

⚐⚐

Ilyana struggled to keep her eyes open during supper. She had spent most of the past five nights reading the runes. She feared trying any other spells, sure the wizards eventually would sense her use of the Power. Although she still hadn't read all the pages of the volume, Ilyana had promised herself this night she would sleep.

"Ilyana!" Master Glaud shouted, his anger radiating across the hall.

Trembling, she stood and walked over to the wizards' end of the table. She bent a knee. "Yes, Master Wizard, what do you require of me?" Ilyana let out her breath; she sensed no Power emanating from him.

"Ilyana, you've been gravely negligent in your duties. I am told by Wizard Teester," Glaud lifted one pudgy, bejeweled hand and pointed to the squinty-eyed Wizard on his right, "that you have fallen asleep during his lessons on several occasions." Ilyana bowed her head, wondering what punishment would be meted out.

"First Apprentice Shtarn," Master Glaud continued, his voice rising, "reports that you've been late for your responsibilities every morn for almost seven days." He paused and Ilyana dared to look up. All five wizards were staring at her with brows furrowed and lips pressed together. But the malevolence she saw in Glaud's piercing green eyes terrified Ilyana into silence.

"Wizard Durn has admitted that you've not been attending him as required." Master Glaud paused and Ilyana found herself wanting nothing more than to be released from the chamber. "After much discussion, Ilyana, we've decided you don't appreciate the honor we bestowed when you were allowed to study at the tower. Since you're so inattentive to your responsibilities as an apprentice, we don't believe there's any hope you'll find in yourself the diligence required of a wizard." Ilyana's eyes opened wider. They were casting her out. She didn't know how to react.

"You're a disgrace to wizardry, Ilyana. Your apprenticeship is withdrawn. You must leave the tower at the morrow's first light. The fees you paid, of course, are forfeit."

"I apologize for neglecting…"

"Silence!" Glaud interrupted her with a shout and a raised hand. "We'll not listen to your excuses."

Unable to speak a word in her own defense, Ilyana stood staring at the wizards until Glaud dismissed her with a wave of his hand. She turned and left the hall, climbing the stairs to her cell. Ilyana should be ashamed — she had just been cast out in disgrace; or angry — what she had paid to study wizardry would have bought five or more apprenticeships at any other guild hall. Instead, the only emotions Ilyana felt were relief and joy.

No longer would she suffer the soldiers' taunts and Shtarn's groping. No more standing on the stairs in the summer's heat or running about at Wizard Durn's beck and call. Ilyana had endured her last lesson with Wizard Teester. Convinced the wizards would never teach her anything about the Magic, she could think of no reason to stay. The price of her apprenticeship wouldn't be forfeit if she succeeded in carrying away the Magic volume and the ruby ring.

Stretched out on her cot, Ilyana fretted about where she would go and how she would support herself. What would Losa have expected of her? As her grandmother had grown older, Ilyana began to believe that Losa's lessons had great purpose, but she had never learned what. Many times Losa had said that four wizards' towers stood in Lowor. Three had been abandoned generations ago. Was Ilyana supposed to bring the Magic to one of the other towers? How could she if she hadn't earned a journey worker's belt?

Ilyana sat up, back straight, chin high. She already knew some Magic. She could study the volume and learn more — enough to serve as a wizard even without guild sanction. She wouldn't, she promised herself, emulate Master Glaud and the others by charging fees to live opulently. She would offer the Magic to any who asked. If she used it to help people, in return would they give her what she needed to survive? Ilyana let that hope calm her.

Before she left Meech, one other matter required her attention. Ilyana lit her candle and thumbed through the volume until she found the spell that had caught her eye two nights past. After rereading it a few times, she crept down the stairs to the next level and stood outside the door to Shtarn's cell. Ilyana whispered the words, backwards, to the spell that restored a man's virility and drew the proper rune, in reverse, upon his door. According to the volume, any spell could be undone this way. Ilyana didn't know what would occur if a spell had never been cast, but she delighted in imagining Shtarn's consternation. Grinning, she returned to her own chamber. Resolved in her vision of her future, hopeful that she prevented Shtarn from assaulting other women, Ilyana slept through the night for the first time in half a moon.

When she sensed dawn's arrival, Ilyana lit the candle and took her haversack from the hook on the wall where it had hung since she arrived in Meech. She dug out her own clothing. After wearing a floor-length apprentice's robe for more than twelve moons, Ilyana's Leerian tunic no longer felt natural. With its short skirts gathered between her legs, her shins were exposed to the weather — and the eyes of every soldier and apprentice who had been ogling her. No matter. Ilyana would find a tailor to make her a gown that would cover her legs. And, she would have rune patterns sewn to the edges of the sleeves and neck. Nothing as elaborate as the wizards wore; mayhap just one color — red, like the ruby.

Ilyana secreted the ruby ring in her purse with her flint, the coins that remained from her inheritance, and the silver betrothal amulet her father had given her mother. The volume was too tall to fit in her haversack, so Ilyana wrapped it in one of the quilts first. It stuck out of the pack a bit, but she hoped it looked as if she had more clothing than would fit. She put her head through the strap and rested it on one shoulder. On the second level, she found food waiting for the apprentices to break their fast. Ilyana crammed as much bread and cheese as would fit next to the wrapped volume in her haversack and slipped some plums and a pear into her purse. The closest of the other three towers, near the borough of Dunt, required at least seven days' journey afoot.

None of the apprentices spoke to Ilyana as she descended the rest of stairs and left the tower. She never saw Shtarn. Two soldiers standing outside the entrance offered to provide her with a place to sleep, for a price. She ignored them. Ilyana headed north on the road toward Meech, her head high and her step light.

Keert and another soldier she had seen about the tower stopped in the road when they saw Ilyana. "Where are you going, Apprentice?" This soldier was shorter and smaller than Keert. His face bore the mark of the pox and his nose had been broken at least once.

"The wizards cast me out." Although Ilyana believed she was better off leaving the tower, her own words cut through her like a knife. She tried to swallow the lump in her throat. "I am no longer a wizard's apprentice."

"You have a very large burden for one who has been disgraced." The soldier's eyes narrowed as he glared at her haversack, the quilt-covered volume protruding from the top.

Despite the summer's heat, a cold chill ran down Ilyana's spine. She clenched one fist behind her back, determined not to tremble before the soldiers. "This is all that I own in the world." Ilyana patted her haversack with her other hand, trying not to seem burdened by its weight. "I spent my entire inheritance on my apprenticeship." Ilyana looked down and bowed her head, hoping she appeared contrite. "All that I carry in here is my clothing, a quilt to sleep on, and some food for my journey."

"I thought you were from Leer? Why are you traveling north?" Last spring, Keert had commented about the way she spoke and, because he had been kind to her, Ilyana had shared that information. Would she now regret the conversation? Although he couldn't have seen more than five and twenty summers, Keert's face already showed the added flesh and mottled color of one who imbibed in too much drink, making it difficult to read his expression.

Ilyana looked up and let a tear fall from her eye. "My family disowned me when I apprenticed as a wizard." Her voice quavered. "Even though I have been cast out, I cannot return home." She fixed her gaze on Keert, hoping the sympathy he had shown her in the past would spare her now. A tumult of emotions inundated Ilyana — fear of the soldiers discovering the volume, her unexpected reaction to speaking of her disgrace, and her uncertainty about her future.

"Where will you go?" Keert's voice expressed concern, but the other soldier still eyed Ilyana's haversack with suspicion.

"I do not know. East, I suppose." Would Keert protect her against one of his own?

"First, I will see what's in your bag." The other soldier reached for the haversack, but Keert pushed his hand away.

"Leave her be, Sark. Don't you think she's suffered enough without you pawing through her clothing? She has no home, no money, and no way to support herself."

"Well, I might be interested in making a contribution on the latter account." Sark ran a lecherous look up and down Ilyana's small frame.

"We're going to be late for our watch." Keert pulled Sark away and Ilyana gave the tall soldier a grateful, tear-filled smile. "Fare well, Ilyana," Keert said over his shoulder. "May you find better fortune elsewhere."

"Thank you, Keert. I will remember your kindness."

Ilyana turned and hurried on her way, passing by the soldiers' barracks without another challenge. As she left the encampment behind, Ilyana took several deep breaths and brought her heartbeat back to a more normal rate. She pulled her braid over her shoulder so the sweat could dry from the back of her neck.

Just before reaching Meech, Ilyana turned east on the road to Thies, the road that would take her to the River Thurs and the borough of Dunt. Although it might be wise to travel further from Meech, Ilyana doubted she had the stamina for a longer journey. At any rate, the tower near Dunt also was the closest to Leer. The headwaters of the same river flowed past the village where she was born.

Ilyana squinted in the bright sunlight, confident that she would find answers to questions that had tormented her all her life in the parchment pages filling her haversack. She would be a wizard. Mayhap not in the eyes of those at Meech. But she would offer the Magic to the people of Dunt. They could judge whether she was worthy of the title.

F. I. Goldhaber

F. I. Goldhaber has been a professional writer for more than twenty years. She spent six years as a reporter and editor at newspapers in three states and then worked as a business writer, editor, and marketing communications consultant for business, government, and not-for-profit entities. A graduate of the University of Washington, F.I. lives in western Oregon.

The story of Ilyana and the Magic continues in the fantasy series, "Magic of Lowor." The first novel *Revenge & Prophecy* should be published in 2005. To learn more about Lowor and when *Revenge & Prophecy* will be available, visit www.lowor.com.

Young at Heart
John Hope

Thomas Smith was always young at heart, just not today. His blistered hands ached, his arthritic knees throbbed, and his eyes were growing heavier and heavier. He retired after yet another long, frustrating day, to his shabby, dull chair that sat lonesome in his drafty house. He leaned his head back on the cracking cushions as his eyes stared, unfocused, at the chipping paint on the ceiling. His right arm swung down to the side of the chair and he grabbed his all-too-familiar liquor bottle. Lifting it to eye level, he cursed at the sight of it being empty; he chucked it to the floor.

Thomas found the energy to lift himself out of the chair and shuffle over to the cigarette-stained table where he had thrown a pile of mail before he sat down. The room was dark and the harsh afternoon glare from a nearby window was dimming, which made it increasingly difficult to decipher between one bill and the next; his eyes ached. Deciding to use his TV's glow for a new source of light, made his way over toward a small end table at the side of his chair. He frowned at the sight of a missing TV remote. He swung his head back and forth, trying to recall where he had last placed it. At last, from the corner of his eye, he spotted it lying on the floor next to a dusty book. Dropping the mail, he walked over and bent down to pick it up. In attempts of pulling himself back up, he began to lose his balance and instinctively grabbed hold of a nearby shelf. The shelf snapped under his weight and every heavy book once resting on the shelf came tumbling down on his feet.

"Dammit!" he cursed. Deciding to leave the books for later, he turned to sit back down in his chair when he stumbled over the largest of the books. He looked down and noticed that the book he was tripping over was an old photo album that looked stunningly familiar. He picked it up and a slight smile almost crossed his face as light dawned on him. "What's this?" he groaned, though he actually recognized it immediately.

He carried the album over to his chair, turned on a lamp that hovered behind the chair, and opened up the album to roughly the end. His heart skipped a beat as a very youthful image of his former wife struck his eye. "Oh, Grace," he sighed as he caressed the faded photo with his weather-beaten hand. He blinked and breathed out a heavy breath. "You were so good to me."

He flipped backward a few pages and came across an even more youthful photo of him surrounded by a few other friends, all of whom were smiling and completely covered in dirt and mud. "Man, those guys," Thomas began speaking to no one. "They were really something." He flipped back a couple more pages and his eyes came across a photo of a young and skinny Thomas Smith standing off to the left side. He stared at the picture closer and noticed a county fair of some sort in the background. "That's odd," he wondered. "I could have sworn I was with Bobby Daniels every time I went to the county...." There was a knock at the door. "...fair," he completed.

He closed the album, and dropped it into his chair as he stood up and slowly staggered to the door. He unlocked the series of bolts and latches to reveal a twelve-year-old boy holding a half-eaten ball of cotton candy.

"Is Scaredy-pants here?" the boy asked innocently.

"Who?" Thomas rather harshly retorted.

"Scaredy-pants?"

"No," he looked over the kid, "And I don't appreciate you kids pulling pranks like this. Do you think I'm some sort of senile idiot? You've got to learn that older people don't like to screw around with things like this!" He slammed the door and sealed it with a bolt lock.

Marching back to his chair, he paused. Just for a second, the boy looked familiar. He could not place how or where he knew the kid, yet he could not shake the feeling.

He finished his trek and plopped down into his chair. Leaning to one side, he pulled out the photo album he had just sat on top of. He gave himself a few minutes to calm back down. Glancing down at the frayed album helped him find some peace. Opening it up again, his tired eyes danced from picture to picture, each photo bringing back one warm, tender feeling after another. Suddenly, another picture caught his attention. This one posed him as an eight-year-old tucked into a sleeping bag in a tent that appeared to have two other empty sleeping bags. The picture appeared familiar but he could not quite place the image with a memory. He wondered why he had two other sleeping bags if he was the only one… there was another knock at the door.

Disgusted, he got up and stomped back over to the door. Unlocking it, he opened to reveal two young boys with flashlights and dark paint under their eyes. "Can Gruesome Ghoul come out to play?" one of the boys asked excitingly.

"Who?" Thomas frowned.

"Gruesome Ghoul," the other responded.

"No. Sorry, I think you have the wrong house. There's no kids here." Thomas closed the door and walked back to his chair.

Sitting down and holding the album in his lap, he puzzled, "Gruesome Ghoul … now where have I heard that?" The name nagged his memory like a catchy song. Still, he opened the photo album once more in hopes that it would eventually come to him.

Flipping from page to page, each picture was both a fresh and new vision and an old warm feeling of his past life. He came across yet another photo that sat with him awkwardly. It was a picture of him sitting alone in a wooden clubhouse, with makeshift doors and shelves in the background. "Now I know I never was in there by myself. It was against club rules." There was a knock at the door.

Getting up, he answered the door. He looked up to see a half-dozen ten-year-old kids standing at his doorstep. At last, it came to him. All the memories, all faces, all the nicknames, all the smells, all the fun, and all of which he had just somehow forgotten, or maybe just misplaced, resurfaced within him. His eyes came back into focus as he looked at the six boys staring back at him. He then took a deep breath and stepped outside a ten-year-old. Thomas Smith was always young at heart.

John Hope

John Hope is an enthusiastic creative writer who tries to break the standard patterns of storytelling from one story to next. He draws inspiration from the world around him, always listening and looking for yet another story idea. Many of his best ideas come introspectively during his daily runs, as his mind meanders down undiscovered paths. "Young at Heart" came to him in December of 2000 as he thought about his own childhood. In a dream, he stepped through a series of anecdotes that flashed past like photographs. When he woke the next morning and sat down at his computer, another short story was born.

"Young at Heart" is his first published story.

The Hunt

Jaylyn Jensen

It was one of those beautiful Indian-summer days that are only found in the upper Midwest. The sun shone brightly, turning the trees into patches of brilliant yellow, punctuated by crimson and dark green. The small stream flowing from the waterfall glistened like a ribbon, and threw off occasional glints as light filtered through the trees surrounding it. The warm breeze rustled the leaves, showing their lighter undersides, causing the trees to sway gently. The breeze also ruffled the blonde hair of the woman who lay dying on the grass in a small clearing of the park.

Her attacker rummaged through her bag, cursing as he found the $5.26 that was all she had brought with her. He looked at the small table that she had set up. He lifted the wine bottle with the homemade label. Mead. He tried a sip, then spit it out. Fucking weird tasting shit! He lifted the small bowl filled with a white substance. Licking his finger he dipped it in, then tasted it. Salt. He threw the bowl aside. He looked down at the table and thought about taking the two knives that sat there, but they were custom jobs, too unique to fence for money. Enraged, he went over to where the woman lay and yanked her head up by the simple expedient of grabbing her hair. "Stupid bitch. Where's your money?" She simply looked at him. "Hell, you ain't even worth fucking. You're too fat! So tell me where the rest of your money is!" He pulled his arm back preparatory to punching her.

"Damn you," she whispered, glaring at him with such ferocity that he paused, mid-swing. "With my last breath I curse you. May you learn what it is like to be prey!" Her head fell to one side, and she went limp. The man lowered her to the ground and checked for a pulse. Finding none he grinned, kicked the body one final time and, whistling a jaunty tune, headed for the parking lot and his pickup.

As he walked out of sight, another man walked out of the trees and over to the young woman's body. Dressed in greens and browns, he'd blended in with the trees and underbrush. Looking down at the body, he shook his head sorrowfully. Then he looked over his shoulder, back into the woods, and waited. He saw a flash of white and smiled. Turning towards the woods, he whistled softly. A dog emerged and approached him tentatively. She was the size of an English setter, and, except for her color (white with red patches around the ears), she looked like one. He knelt down and she came up to him, still unsure. He reached out and scratched behind her ears, smoothing the red fur there. She looked up at him, then leaned against him, accepting the caress. He continued to pet her, running his hand along her head and back.

"There, there," the man soothed, still petting her. The dog looked at the body, looked up at him and growled. The man laughed. "Yes, you may lead this hunt." He rose and bowed formally to the body lying in front of him. "Thank you my Lady, long has it been since we have had new prey." He motioned to the dog and together they went into the trees.

Phil, the young woman's killer, took the five bucks, bought some beer and spent the rest of the night drinking. He really didn't need the money, he was working full time, he just got off on terrifying women. If anything, he wished that she had struggled more, and lasted longer. He stumbled into his apartment at midnight, missing the news story about the young woman who had died in a remote area of a local park.

That night Phil had a very weird, very real dream. He dreamed that he was a ten-point buck walking through a forest. He was strutting around, looking for other bucks to challenge, when he heard a faint howl. All senses on alert, he looked around warily. The howl sounded closer. Feeling the first traces of fear, he started to trot away from the howl, only to hear the sound of many dogs baying. Realizing that they had gotten his scent, he leaped over a fallen log and ran as fast as he could away from the dogs. He could hear them getting closer and closer. Then, suddenly, his alarm clock rang and he sat up in his own bed, heart pounding, drenched in sweat. He looked around, half expecting to see the forest, and relaxed when he realized he was in his own room.

That day Phil kept glancing around nervously as he cleaned the big office building, unable to shake the feeling of being hunted that had followed him out of the dream. After work, Phil and a bunch of his buddies went to their local hangout to drink beer and shoot some pool. At midnight, drunk and feeling no pain, he made his way to his apartment and passed out on the bed, not even able to get undressed.

The dream he had was the same, only the dogs got even closer before his alarm went off. Feeling exhausted, Phil went to work, then went home and drank himself senseless. It did not stop the dream. The dogs kept getting closer, and he tried to sleep less and less each night. One day, exhausted, he fell asleep during his break. His boss happened to walk by, an hour later, and suspended Phil for three days, warning him that if he did it again, he'd be fired. Phil went home, hoping to finally get some sleep, only to have the dream again. This time, he saw flashes of white in the forest before he woke up to hear the phone ringing. It was 4:30.

"Hey, Phil!" It was Mark, one of his buddies. "Want to go to the club tonight?"

"Why?"

"They got a psychic doing a show. She's 'sposed to be real good."

"Sure, I'll go." Phil knew that Mark was interested in psychic shit, even though he tried to hide it. Besides, Phil would do anything to keep his mind off of the dream. "What time?"

"I'll pick you up at seven"

The hours between 4:30 and 7:00 were the longest Phil had ever spent. He kept hearing the dogs. Even though he was awake, he kept hearing the damned barking. Hell, maybe the psychic would know what was going on.

Mark and Phil walked into the nightclub after paying the $5.00 cover. They got a table right next to the stage and started off with a couple of beers. After their second beer, Mark turned to Phil.

"Man, you ain't looking so good. What's up?"

"Nothing, just been having weird dreams lately."

Determined to make conversation, Mark continued. "You hear about the woman who died last week? Cops are still wondering what the hell happened."

"Oh yeah? So what's so strange about that?"

"Turns out she was a witch. You know, one of those New Age freaks. She even worked with the cops on a couple of cases."

Phil turned white, remembering the woman's dying words. Mark was about to ask what was wrong when the show started. The psychic, Madam Zorta, wearing bright silver and gold lamé robes and a turban, did the usual shtick. She'd say something like, "There's someone in the audience looking for a job. Don't worry, you'll have one in two weeks."

After the show, and two more beers apiece, Phil and Mark slipped the guy guarding the door a twenty and went backstage to Madam Zorta's dressing room.

"Come in" she responded in a low musical voice as they knocked. They walked in, and stopped in surprise. Madam Zorta was gorgeous. She hadn't looked that way on stage — her makeup had made her look fifty! She looked up, then smiled at the look on their faces.

"And what may Madam Zorta do for you?"

Mark looked at Phil, then back at her. "My friend here has been having weird dreams. We were wondering if maybe you could help him out."

Madam Zorta looked Phil up and down. "I charge forty dollars for a private reading."

Phil reached into his pocket and peeled two twenties off of a wad of cash, then handed them to her.

She took the cash, put it on the dressing table, then walked over to a small table. "Sit there," she commanded pointing at the chairs opposite.

When the two men were seated she lit a candle next to the crystal ball that sat in the center of the table. "Be quiet until I say that you can speak."

Both men nodded, then watched in fascination as she began to breathe deeply, staring at the flame reflected in the crystal. It was silent for a moment, then she began to gasp for air. Acting as if she were fighting someone, she leapt out of her chair and backed away from the two men.

"Here!" She yelled, throwing the two twenties back at Phil. "Take it. I want no money from a walking dead man."

Phil grabbed the money as Mark went over to the woman, grabbed her arms, and shook her. "What are you talking about? What's wrong with Phil?"

Madam Zorta broke Mark's grip. She looked at him, then over at Phil. "The man's been cursed. By the gods. In your dreams, you are hunted, right? You are hunted by dogs and you are a deer or moose or something like that?" Phil's dropped jaw gave her the answer to her question. "You will live until they catch you. When they catch you in your dreams, you will die. Now go, I must cleanse this place so they do not catch my scent too." She turned back towards Mark. "Stay away from him, or they may start hunting you. Now go."

The men left the room as if shot from a cannon. They made their way to where Mark's car was parked, not noticing the dusky-skinned man, dressed in green and brown, who was following them, a white dog at his side. They got in and Mark started the engine, then turned to Phil.

"You don't believe her do you?"

"No, I guess not. But how'd she know about my dreams?"

"I dunno. Lucky guess I 'spose," Mark replied, wondering himself. "So now what?"

"Let's stop by the liquor store, get a 24-pack of beer and go get drunk."

"Sounds good to me."

Behind them, the man walking the dog smiled. More prey had just presented itself. It would be a good hunt.

They went back to Phil's apartment, got plastered and passed out in the living room with the TV on. Phil had the same dream, only this time, he actually saw one of the dogs before he woke up, and stumbled to the bathroom. When he came back into the living room, Mark was thrashing around and yelling.

"Hey, man. Wake up!" Phil shook him by the shoulder.

"Whaa? Phil? Where am I?" Mark looked around, half-asleep. Shaking his head he looked around again.

"You musta been having a nightmare," Phil said. "You were yelling in your sleep."

"A nightmare? Yeah, I guess it was. But it was so real. I was walking in the woods and all of a sudden I heard dogs barking. I knew they were hunting me. I don't know how I knew that but I knew. So I ran and ran and then you were shaking me." Mark looked up, and saw the horror on Phil's face. "She was right, wasn't she? That's the dream you've been having, isn't it?"

Phil nodded. "I saw one of the dogs this time. They keep getting closer and closer."

Mark swore under his breath. "So what are we gonna do?"

"You go back to that Madam Zorta. See if she can, what'd she call it? Cleanse you."

"I can't. It was her last night there. I don't know where she went."

"Call the club. Or go see another psychic. Maybe they can help you."

"What about you?"

"Nothin's gonna stop them from getting me. It's too late."

Mark tried to persuade Phil to go with him, but Phil refused. Finally Mark left in search of another psychic, as a call to the club had confirmed the fact that Madam Zorta was gone.

Unable to sit in his apartment any longer, Phil drove to the park where the girl had died. Walking near the creek, Phil was startled by the sound of a dog barking close by. He kept on walking. He knew that people often brought their dogs to the park to be exercised. The dog stopped barking, then started again, closer. Phil turned towards the sound, and saw a white dog running towards him through the trees, the dog he had seen in his dreams. Turning away, he ran along the stream, towards the small falls and rapids area, about 200 feet away. About twenty feet from the falls, Phil tripped over a root and fell to his hands and knees. Looking behind him, he saw a pack of the white dogs, closing in on him fast. Getting up, he ran to the falls and started climbing the 25-foot bluff. Looking down, he saw the dogs, silent now, jumping up and down at the base of the cliff. Phil was five feet away from the top when he heard a hunting horn. Looking down, he saw a man come up to the dogs and look up at him.

"Help me!" Phil yelled. "The dogs want to kill me!"

"No, they don't," the man replied in a calm voice to the panicked Phil. "At least not all of them. The only one who does is that one."

Phil's gaze followed the man's pointing finger. The indicated dog sat down and licked its chops. Then he blinked in surprise, for behind the dog was a shape he recognized. He could see through it to the trees beyond, but it was definitely the girl he had murdered.

Phil looked back at the man. "Please, I don't wanna die. What can I do?"

The man smiled unpleasantly. "You can do nothing." With that, the man pulled a crossbow off his back, cocked it, placed the quarrel in the groove, and fired at Phil.

Phil ducked as the quarrel passed over his head, then screamed as he felt his grip loosen. The last sound he heard was the crunch of bones as his neck snapped.

The female hound, Phil's victim, came over to him, sniffed then sat down and howled. The man came up to her and, when she had stopped howling, patted her on the head. "Your hunt is over. Go to the Lady." With that, the female hound faded away. The man then whistled sharply, and a male hound came up to him, cowering at his feet. "You will stay with the pack until you find us new prey. When the prey is killed, you may continue your journey to the afterlife. Your companions either refused to find us prey, or could not find us prey." The hounds cowered as he waved at them. "That is why they still hunt. As will you, if you do not find us something to hunt. Do you understand?" The hound wagged its tail in confirmation. "Good, now find us new prey!"

The police responded to a call from a hiker in the park about a body at the foot of the falls. After an extensive investigation, they deemed it an accident; another stupid idiot climbing where he wasn't supposed to. Mark, hearing of his friend's death on the evening news, was glad that he had found an occult bookstore and had learned how to cleanse and shield himself.

That night, Phil's boss had a dream.

Jaylyn Jensen

Jaylyn Jensen started reading SF&F at the age of 13 when someone gave her an Andre Norton novel. She's been hooked ever since. When she moved from St. Louis to the Twin Cities, she was introduced to Minicon (a local SF&F convention). She dedicates this story to Paul, in memory of the very interesting conversations they had. In addition, she thanks E.D. for editorial suggestions. She is currently working on a novel.

This is her first published short story.

The Sunspot
Diane Masiello

Connie could barely keep her eyes on the road. The glare of the sun was blinding and she'd forgotten to put on her sunglasses. Her blue sedan slowed as she rustled through her gray canvas shoulder bag searching for them. A red pickup roared past on the right and cut her off. "Redneck," she mumbled. She finally found the glasses and drew them out by one earpiece. They snapped in two. Connie sighed in exasperation. Now she'd be squinting all the way to work, and she'd probably have a headache all day.

Traffic was heavy this morning. Then again, it had been heavy for a long time now. Not like when she Dave first moved to this small Florida town. Back then it had been mostly citrus groves and cow pastures. New construction in the area had brought so many people the roads could barely handle them. She sighed and watched the cars change lanes, as if getting ahead of one car would get them to work that much sooner.

Out of the corner of her eye she saw a little sunspot, the kind of light her cats liked to chase in the morning. She smiled, remembering the way Dave would torment them by using sunlight reflecting off his watch to make a sunspot that would roll around like a crazy thing. They had both reveled in the cats' dismay as it moved wildly about, ungraspable beneath their paws. As traffic slowed Connie focused her attention on the sunspot, and noticed that it roiled in a similar way now. But where was it coming from?

She checked her wrist and noticed she had forgotten her watch. Yet another missing accessory, and certainly not the source of the reflection. Traffic began to move again. The sunspot swirled and swiveled all over the backseat. She did a mental check of what she was wearing. Although her green flowered blouse and skirt had lovely buttons, they were covered with material — not a piece of metal showing. She thought of her earrings. She looked in the mirror to see the pearl floral post earrings Dave had given her on their last anniversary. Maybe it was the diamond on her ring. She looked down at her finger and pain pierced her chest. The diamond was gone.

She had stopped wearing it two weeks after he died, altering his simple golden band to fit her finger. It was too painful to wear the engagement ring he'd had custom made for her more than ten years ago. No more diamonds for me, she had decided. But the ring had been such a part of her that she often forgot it was gone, just as she often forgot he was gone. She fought back tears. It's been over a year since the accident. I have to get past this. Yet little things like this, small remembrances, still had the power to sear her soul.

The radio blared a happy little song and she leaned to turn it off. She didn't want to be happy now. She looked over her shoulder to see if there was room for her to change lanes and noticed the sunspot hopping across the back of the car in time to the cheery music. She left the radio alone and watched as the spot bounced along the ceiling then twirled above the rearview mirror.

The song on the radio changed to a ballad. The sunspot's movement slowed until it was a small shimmer. She realized that she was spending more time watching the spot than the road and quickly drew her attention back to the highway. Every so often she glanced up at the spot. It waved and gleamed all the way to work. It wasn't until she'd parked under a big oak in the school parking lot that she realized her eyes hadn't hurt for quite a while. The day had become overcast.

The realization jolted her. Was she going crazy? How could there be a sunspot without sun? She watched it bop along to another upbeat song across the passenger side's sun visor. Feeling like her cat, she reached up to cover the spot. It didn't disappear and didn't shine on top of her hand, either. Under her palm the glow brightened until it shone through her fingers. Little wings fluttered against her palm. It tickled, the same way lightning bugs used to when she caught them as a child. But could a lightning bug be in Florida, in January, in daylight?

Her first impulse was to let it go, get out of the car, and walk away. She was already late and had a lot of planning to do. Maybe it was because she was tired, or sad, or because she longed for a little adventure. Maybe it was because she needed some magic. For whatever reason, she didn't move her hand. She ignored her brain's pat explanations which she had accepted all her life when seeing something odd or mysterious. Under her trembling palm the light intensified until it was like a little part of the sun inside her car. She opened her fingers and peered inside.

The brilliance blinded her. Despite the pain she looked past the radiance, into the light, and saw a shape. She could make out arms. Then legs. Long, green hair flowed over a well-muscled chest and reached to the small leaf that covered a lower torso. Gold-threaded gossamer wings pressed tightly against a body that was a rich yellow, the yellow of the first grapefruits of the season that grew in her yard. She couldn't see any eyes. The light was too bright.

She clapped her hand back down and felt the fluttering again. I can't be seeing this, she thought. This is nonsense. There must be a reasonable explanation. It's just a bug. She nodded to herself. It's easier if it's a bug, easier to forget all this. So let go. Let it go. Let me go. I want to go!

Then she heard it clearly. That little voice in her head wasn't her at all. It came from the creature under her hand. A fairy. It had to be a fairy. She had read enough about them to know. And one was right here. She had caught a fairy.

The fluttering stopped and the creature let out a low moan. She lifted her hand slightly and peeked in. The figure settled like a fallen leaf. His light dimmed and he sat cross-legged, arms supporting him from behind his back, wings folded down. He stared at her with deeply shining eyes that were the same forest green as his hair.

"All right then," he said. "You caught me. Now you know I'm real."

She could feel her own eyes widen.

"Yes, I know," he continued. "It's hard to believe. It can't be true. Fairies don't exist."

"No," Connie corrected the creature. "I do believe. I know it's true. You do exist. I came to terms with that a minute ago. I'm just admiring your coloring. I always thought...."

"Yes, yes," he replied. "I know. You always thought fairies were gossamer, or maybe pink, or looked just like people with creamy peach skin."

"Well," Connie began, but was interrupted again.

"Well, *we* don't. Not here. In Europe, yes. And they do get most of the press. But here we're different."

"I see," she said. "Here you look like ripe grapefruit."

"Yes. Most tropical fairies have my coloring, or are bright orange or green. After all, we're citrus fairies. You can't go hiding among oranges, limes, lemons and grapefruits looking like a strawberry, can you?"

"I guess not." Connie wondered at herself having this conversation with a fairy. "What's your name?" she asked.

"I don't really have one. Not in the human sense. You're all so intent on naming things, as if it helps control them. We fairies recognize one another by our looks, call to one another by imitating the distinctive wing flutter each of us develops, kind of like a voice. When I want to camouflage myself, I project as a sunspot. So you can call me that, Connie." He smugly looked at her as he said her name.

"You know my name?"

"Of course I know your name," he snapped. "I've been in your yard all my life — over a hundred years — though it only became your yard when you built that monstrosity of a house. I've spent the last ten years of my life avoiding you, your cats, your grapefruit picker." His eye-rolling, disgusted expression made her laugh.

"You've been around all that time?"

"Of course. I live in your grapefruit tree, one of the few that weren't cut down when they turned the citrus grove into a housing complex. I stayed to guard my tree and keep it healthy."

"Oh," was all Connie could think to say. This was a lot to take in at once. But she wasn't really surprised. She always thought there was something special about that tree. It was the one the cats loved to climb, the one she would find herself staring at when her mind drifted from her work. It always yielded the juiciest fruit. She smiled at Sunspot, thinking about the sweet fruit of his tree. He suddenly seemed like an old friend.

"So," she said, "what are you doing in my car?"

He turned in her hand and pointed to the bag of grapefruit she had brought for the school secretary. "You got me. I couldn't believe it, but you finally got me. I'd been avoiding your hands for years, but you caught me off guard. You were particularly quiet this morning." He looked at her accusingly. "You scooped me into that smelly bag!"

She smiled. "Sorry." He looked so downtrodden she wanted to say more, but she couldn't think of anything.

"It's all right. I'm just getting old, that's all. And I have a lot on my mind."

She thought of how similar their situations were. The stone of depression rolled against her heart again, but she pushed it away. "So now the question is, I guess, what do I do with you?"

"Well," he said, "whatever it is, don't leave me in the car with the windows up. I only let you see me because I was afraid I'd die of the heat locked in this car all day."

"Oh," Connie said sweetly, "and I thought you just wanted the pleasure of my company. Do you want to come to work with me?"

"Better than dying of heatstroke. But you should know I'll just be a sunspot on your desk. You'll look ridiculous if you try to talk to me in front of people, and you'll probably draw a lot of attention." He looked past her head and pointed out the driver's-side window. "Like now."

Connie turned to see her colleague, Tim, standing outside the car. He moved to look in, then turned away. He had always been one of her best friends in the math department. She liked his green eyes and shy smile, and admired his love for teaching. In the months after Dave's death he was the only one who could come close to making her laugh. But when he asked her to dinner last week, she couldn't bring herself to go.

He wasn't moving away from her car. He had probably been watching her talk into the palm of her hand for the past five minutes. Even though he was a good friend, she doubted he'd believe her if she told him the truth. She had to come up with some explanation for her odd behavior. She reached into her overstuffed gray bag and took out the tape recorder she used to leave memos for herself. With her other hand she motioned the fairy into her bag.

He disappeared with a flash. She zipped her bag shut but left a small crack for ventilation, then got out of the car.

Concern shadowed Tim's eyes. "Hi, Connie," he said. His voice was tentative.

"Good morning," she replied cheerily. She waved the recorder in the air. "You know, this was the best idea you ever had. Thank you for encouraging me to buy one! I don't know what I'd do without it."

His eyes lost their worried look, and he sighed as if he'd been holding his breath.

"Is everything okay, Tim?"

"Yes, everything is just... well, um...." He shook his head. "It's just that when I saw you in your car talking to yourself... I should've known it was the tape recorder. I guess I've just been kind of worried about you, so I jumped to some conclusions."

"No need to check me into the crazy house yet!" She laughed. Her ruse had worked.

"Well then," he replied, "since you have no plans for relocation, how about going out to dinner and dancing with me Friday night?"

Relief left her in a rush. She couldn't deal with this now. Sunspot rustled in her bag and she hiked the strap higher onto her shoulder to keep Tim from noticing the movement. "I'm not ready yet, Tim."

His face fell in disappointment. But she wasn't ready to start dating. It was too soon. Her stomach began to ache.

He looked into her eyes, pulled a piece of paper and a pen from his back pocket, and wrote numbers in large, clear print. "I never gave you my new phone number after I moved. I know you're still going through a rough time, but I really want to be there for you. We don't have to talk about this at work anymore, and I'm not going to keep bothering you with invitations. But when you're ready, Connie, call me."

She took the piece of paper. "Thanks." The ache in her stomach intensified, and she couldn't control the heat seeping into her face. Hoping he wouldn't see her blush, she tucked the card into the pocket of her skirt and turned toward her classroom. Her heart beat almost as fast as the wings fluttering against her purse. She wondered how eager Tim would be to go on a date with a grieving widow who saw fairies.

∂≈

Even though it was after midnight, Connie was wide awake as she got into her car. Her body trembling, she felt more alive than she'd felt since Dave's death. Ever since Sunspot had brought her to visit what he called his "country cousins," who lived in one of the last remaining citrus groves, she had been going there almost every night to see them.

This night was no different. She drove ten miles, then parked on the side of the road where the grass had grown so high it hid her car. She took a lawn chair and boom box out of the trunk and started off toward the center of the grove. When she came to the clearing that Sunspot had shown her, she set the radio down, turned the volume up and pressed play. She sat down on the chair to watch. As the tape of rhythmic mambo music started to roll, the trees began to gleam with little dots of orange and yellow lights.

They rose out of the branches and swirled around her, bouncing giddily to the drums. She could just make out their little bodies as they flew in front of her eyes. She saw two fairies clasp hands and twirl in a circle; she saw three converge together and gyrate their wings and feet and heads in a tumble of limbs. Some danced alone, their heads swirling around, their wings fluttering so fast they were a blur. The air teemed with light, with a warm, loving, primal glow.

"Magic," she thought. She hadn't realized she'd said it aloud until she heard a voice respond.

"Oh yes, my dear. This is a magical place."

Connie whirled around in her seat to see an old woman sitting in a lawn chair behind her. She was dressed in overalls and sneakers, with a yellow scarf covering her hair. Her face was lit by the glow from the fairy dance, and her eyes sparkled. In those eyes Connie saw signs of a kindred spirit. This woman posed no threat to her, or her secret.

"I'm Connie," she said, dragging her chair beside the woman.

"I'm Betty." They shook hands gently.

"How long have you known?" Connie motioned to the flurry of lights trembling before their eyes, tirelessly dancing.

"All my life," Betty responded. "This was my family's grove."

Not daring to breathe, Connie looked at Betty's face and saw a youthful gleam resurrected by magic — the look that had appeared on Connie's face in the month she had been coming to the grove. "So you've had this here, you've seen this, since you were little?"

"Yes," Betty responded. "My grandpa and grandma brought me out here when I was three to see them dance. It's my first memory. Back then we didn't have these portable radios." A sturdy, work-worn finger pointed to the boom box. "We just sat and watched them swirl. They made their own music back then. Their wings hummed louder and more melodically than anything I've heard since. They could still do that now, I suppose. They just don't."

"Oh, they have a reason," Connie said. "Their music draws people, and they don't want to be seen anymore. When I play this, people think it's a bunch of kids having a party in the grove and don't investigate. But fairy music sounds different. It draws attention. The fairies don't want any more attention — they've had enough of it, seeing how it's mostly been bad. At least, that's what my grapefruit fairy says."

"Oh!" Betty laughed. "You have one of those curmudgeonly old fellows!" Connie laughed along with her. "Quite a handful, I'll bet."

"Yes. He is a bit woeful and grumpy."

"That's what happens when they go *suburban*!" Betty spat it like it was a dirty word. "Start seeing themselves as solitary guardians rather than part of the Dance."

Connie nodded. Sounded like Sunspot to her. "He is quite a handful, but he brought me here."

"And he proved there is magic in this world," Betty finished for her. They nodded together. Betty leaned over conspiratorially and whispered, "But you always knew, didn't you?"

"Oh yes," Connie whispered back. "But everyone made me feel…."

"Silly for believing," Betty concluded. "I was lucky that way. My grandparents knew of the magic in this land. They made sure I never doubted it. My parents, too. It's my children and grandchildren. They're the ones who don't believe."

"My husband never believed, and my neighbors don't either. If my parents did, they never let on."

"Such a shame, really." Betty gestured to the swirling forms, and Connie basked in the warmth of their glow. "Because believing is, well, it makes things so much lighter, don't you think?"

"Absolutely. Fairies don't answer any of those big questions about life and death, but the very fact that they exist makes me believe answers are out there somewhere."

The two women sat in silence and watched the twinkling ones. The air was thick with them now — more than Connie had ever seen before. Each spot was filled with an orange, yellow or green glow blotting out all the darkness. The dancing was becoming more frenetic. Even Sunspot was here, which was unusual. After he introduced her to the grove he hadn't returned, claiming he had too much to do around his tree. But tonight he was glowing brightly, dancing as wildly as the others. She was glad to provide the music for the party.

"How long have *you* known?" Betty's voice gently broke the silence.

"About a month," Connie replied, "But I haven't seen you here before. Why?"

Betty sighed. "It's gotten harder to make my way out here lately. Harder to drive down from the house, to walk from the truck to the grove, harder to do most everything, actually." She paused, and Connie turned to look at her face. When their eyes met, Betty continued, "I had to come out here tonight."

Connie felt cold in the pit of her stomach. "Why?" she asked, though she didn't think she wanted to know the answer. "What's so special about tonight?"

"Oh, child," Betty began. There was a tangible sadness in her voice. Even the fairies slowed their pace, as if her anguish made the air too heavy on their wings. "Tonight is their last dance."

Blackness threatened to overtake Connie as all the sounds and sights of the grove faded away. She pulled herself back from the panicked darkness and asked, hoping for an answer different from the one she suspected to be true, "Why is it their last dance?"

"Because none of this will be here tomorrow." Betty gestured to the edge of the grove where Connie could just make out the shapes of backhoes and bulldozers looming in the darkness.

The music stopped playing. The fairies stopped dancing. Connie held her breath, thinking Betty's words had ended the party. The tape player clicked as it turned the tape over. The music began again and the dancing resumed, as frenetic as ever.

"They sold the land." Both women said it at the same time.

"I couldn't stop them," Betty explained. "I tried, but they wouldn't listen. I had signed the land over years ago when they started managing the grove. The money was so good, and they couldn't see the fairies...."

"They're tearing it down tomorrow?"

Betty nodded.

"So tonight...." Connie turned back to the flashing, swirling array of lights.

Betty's eyes glistened. "Tonight they say good-bye."

"Are they all going to leave?" Connie sounded like a lost little girl; Betty must have heard it the same way. She put her hand on Connie's shoulder.

"Some may stay, if their trees don't get cut down. They can live like your family fairy, a very solitary life." Betty sniffed back tears that shook her voice. "But most will go."

"So we'll never see this again." Once more, they spoke in unison. Connie knew they'd said it to convince themselves it was true, to make themselves believe there was nothing they could do. Connie's chest tightened. She blinked back tears to clear her eyes, so she could see what she would never see again.

She watched the fairies dance, trying to memorize every movement. The fairies, who had never really paid any mind to Connie's presence before, responded to the intensity of her gaze. Three of them, along with Sunspot, broke away from the large group and flew to Connie. Four others went to Betty. Their little hands picked at the women's skin, and tiny voices spoke. "Friends," they said. "Dance with us."

Betty immediately rose and approached the nimbus of light the fairies had made with their bodies. Connie held back. "I don't know," she said, looking at Sunspot. He let go of her sleeve and flew up so her eyes were level with his.

"Connie." He said her name with uncharacteristic gentleness, and her eyes met his. "Even solitary guardians need to come out and join the dance sometimes, or we begin to forget who we are, and why we're here." Tears spilled down her cheeks. His wings fluttered against her face to wipe them away. The other fairies rose to her eye level and repeated, "Friend. Dance with us."

She let them lead her toward the light, which opened for her like a shimmering cloak. She knew Betty was in there, but couldn't see her through the gleaming beams of limbs, hair, faces and eyes that surrounded her. Still, she wasn't afraid. She was at peace. She closed her eyes and welcomed their heat against her face, the fluttering of wings against her body. She began to sway, slowly undulating to the music. Waves of sound pulsed through her. She opened her eyes to see fairies paint glowing trails of footprints all over her. She breathed in the scent of orange blossoms and grapefruit juice, lime and lemon scent, and hoped that the sun would never rise and she would stay like this, surrounded by magic, dancing forever.

Eventually the sky began to shine with a light of its own and the dancing stopped. Three fairies flitted away and shut off the music. Others led the women back to their seats. Connie and Betty sat down, exhausted and exhilarated at the same time. The glowing figures hugged, kissed, smiled, waved their wings. Then they flew off to their trees. Had they gone to pack for the trip? Connie wondered. What sort of things do fairies own?

Neither woman spoke but they sat together through the dawn. At eight the workmen came. The noise of rumbling motors cut the gentle air. Connie helped Betty up from her chair and walked her back to the side of the road where her gray pickup waited next to Connie's sedan. She put Betty's chair in the bed of the pickup and helped Betty into the cab.

Betty started the truck and gunned the motor loudly, but it wasn't enough to drown out the sound of a bulldozer wrenching up the roots of the first tree. She rolled down her window and looked at Connie. "I can't stay to watch this, honey," she said. Tears streamed down her face. "It's just too much."

Connie nodded and stepped back from the truck as Betty rolled the window up. The wheels caught and kicked up dirt as she sped away. Connie stood in the dust, waving, trying to hold back her own tears. She turned to the grove, where a large yellow claw was ripping up roots.

Over the din of the motors, a steady hum began. A set of twinkling lights whirled toward Connie, and before she could blink she found fairies on her shoulders, in her hair, on her hands. She giggled, and at the sound the fairies fluttered their wings and began swooping through the air.

"What's all this?" Connie asked.

Sunspot flew up to her face. "These are my traveling companions. I asked them to wait for me while I said good-bye."

"Good-bye?"

"Yes, Connie. Good-bye."

"But, but why?" She felt the tears that she had fought all night washing over her face. "What about your tree? What about me? You stayed last time, when they cut down the grove. Why are you leaving now?"

"These are the last of my kind, Connie. When the other group left, it was okay. Some of my family and friends moved to this grove. I still had them nearby to visit when I felt lonely, or at festival time." The fairies swooped around, as if the very mention of a festival had set their bodies dancing. She cherished their movements, her eyes following their light. Sunspot loudly cleared his throat. The fairies settled down and she turned her attention back to him.

"Now they're all leaving," he said.

"All of them? Betty said some might stay."

"No," Sunspot sighed. "They've decided they can't watch the destruction anymore — it just hurts too much. While I found I can live as a solitary fairy, I certainly can't live cut off from all the others of my kind. So I have to go, too."

Connie wiped the tears from her face. She leaned forward and gave Sunspot a small kiss on his green head. He glowed brighter and brighter and his eyes gleamed a deeper green.

"I understand why you have to go," Connie said, "but I'll miss you."

"I'll miss you too, Connie. But I have to get back into the

Dance. And I think you do, too." He floated up to her cheek and returned her kiss. His feathery lips against her skin tickled. She giggled at the touch, then felt the weight of grief, fear and loneliness ease a bit.

"It sure was nice to dance again," she mused aloud.

Sunspot floated to her ear and whispered, "I know it won't be as magical as dancing with us, but that Tim guy didn't sound like he'd be the worst dancer in the world."

"No, he isn't, actually. I've seen him at faculty parties. He dances much better than I do, anyway."

"So, maybe let him teach you a step or two," Sunspot offered.

Connie remembered Tim's number in her skirt pocket. "I think I will."

The fairies began to flutter anxiously, the hum from the orange grove intensified. The fairies rose together in a vibrant twinkle, like a giant, gleaming, yellow-and-orange rainbow. Sunspot and his companions each gently touched Connie before they took flight, waving as they sped to join the gleaming arch. She waved back; then watched them fly away, fast and far.

The workers never saw the rainbow. They were too busy watching the beautiful woman who stood by the side of the road, sparkling in sunlight, staring at the sky and swaying to a beat only she could hear.

Diane Masiello

Diane Masiello is an Assistant Professor of English at the University of Tampa. She lives in Florida with her husband, John, and her two cats, Demi and Allegra. She wrote this story in tribute to the orange groves that builders tore down around her home. Every spring, she still misses the magical smell of the orange blossoms.

World Without End
Kenra J. Miller

August 8, 1995

Dr. Addison sat on a stool and ran his hands through his thinning red hair. How could this happen?

The Enforced Sterility Injection should've been the saving of mankind and the planet. Now after fifteen years of research they'd found a flaw. It'd taken that long for the chemicals in the injection to eat away at the genes that controlled the aging process.

Fifteen years ago, everyone had been given the ESI. Each country's government would control population through the use of ESI and euthanasia. Once they felt their population was at an "acceptable" level, they would begin re-population using scientifically engineered test-tube babies.

The world wouldn't be able to wait, they needed to start breeding their children now. Within six years, every human being on the planet would be dead. Dr. Addison picked up the phone.

"Mr. King, please.

"Steve, I've got some bad news for you. We found a flaw in the genes. It takes the chemicals in the injection fifteen years to break down and start attacking the genes that control aging.

"I don't know if it can be corrected! We just finished checking our results!

"Yes, of course. I'll have everybody in the cafeteria at seven p.m.

"I understand. Good-bye."

After hanging up the phone, Dr. Addison reached for the

intercom switch. "Your attention please. There'll be a staff meeting at seven p.m. tonight in the cafeteria. Attendance is mandatory. Thank you."

At seven-thirty everyone was in the cafeteria drinking coffee and talking quietly.

Suddenly a strange voice was heard coming from the intercom. "It's checkout time!"

Everyone stood frozen. What was going on?

A brilliant wave of heat and flames lit the night sky. An impeccably dressed figure basked in the glow of the dazzling inferno. At the sound of approaching sirens, he slid into his Mercedes and accelerated into the darkness.

⇗⇘

August 2, 2000

Dr. Connors hurried down the hallway. Smoothing his rumpled lab coat he stopped at the receptionist's desk. "I need to see Mr. King!"

The blonde behind the desk didn't look up from the computer. "He's in a conference and doesn't wish to be disturbed."

"We'll have to see about that," he said.

The receptionist pushed a button on her desk.

As he touched the doorknob, a jolt of electricity bit his hand. "Eileen, this is urgent!" he yelled as he cradled his hand against his narrow chest.

"I'm sure it is, but you know the rules."

A voice erupted from the intercom. "Eileen, send Dr. Conners in and turn off your ray gun please."

Eileen pushed the button and motioned for Dr. Conners to go in.

Facing him from behind the desk was a bald-headed man with a face that looked like it'd been chiseled out of granite.

"What's so important it couldn't wait until our meeting tomorrow morning?"

"Before I get to that, answer a question. Is it just your office you have wired or is it the whole complex?" John asked.

"I didn't get where I am today by being a nice guy. Sometimes it pays to listen at keyholes."

"I got the autopsy results back on the Capuchin monkeys we injected. Of the original ten injected twenty years ago, four have died. The other six are also showing signs of premature aging. There's a fatal flaw in the injection!"

"Do the autopsies again. You know if word of this leaks out, we'll have serious problems on our hands."

"Let's get something straight Steve. I told you twenty years ago the ESI needed more research. You put it on the market anyway! Now it may start killing off the entire population of the planet. With the government enforcing mandatory euthanasia at forty, mankind could very well be extinct in another year!"

"We both know euthanasia was a good idea," Steve said. "It has been medically proven that after forty the mind and body deteriorate. By getting rid of the deadwood we keep our planet from being sucked dry of all its natural resources. It was a good idea to pass that law and you know it."

"We don't have much time John, we were injected too!"

"Get back to the lab, check the autopsy results and get back to me."

After listening to make certain John had left, Steve picked up the phone and dialed.

"Aaron, we've got a problem. He found out. I'm making him do the autopsies again. Replace his computers with new ones tonight. Find a landfill and bury the old ones.

"We already discussed this. I don't care about a cure. We don't need it or him anymore; we have other options now. Give the information to the media. By tomorrow morning he'll be on his way to the Crematorium." Without waiting to hear anymore, Steve hung up and dialed another number.

"Good morning Jill, is he in?" Steve asked. "Would you put me through please?" After exchanging small talk Steve got to the point. "Mr. President, I'm calling about that problem I spoke with you about the other night. I think he needs to be picked up right away. I assure you, he's totally out of control. Thank you Mr. President."

Steve cradled the phone and relaxed into his deeply padded chair.

Years ago the world had been desperate for an answer to

poverty, the serious depletion of the Earth's natural resources and overpopulation.

Euthanasia had been a step in the right direction, but it was to little too late. People had gotten angry when the law was passed, but as parents watched their children starve, life was brought into perspective fast.

When a research firm headed by Dr. John Conners had discovered the Enforced Sterilization Injection, it had given the world a new lease on life. The injection attacked human fertility genes and caused permanent sterility. A law was passed mandating that everyone get the injection including newborns.

Steve had been head of Marketing and Development at the time. Due to his unlimited wealth and power Steve had been able to coerce the FDA into putting their seal of approval on it.

Steve gathered a group of the world's most prominent scientists to do further testing on the ESI. They'd isolated the flaw five years ago. When they found it, they signed their own death warrant. The scientists had gone up in a blaze of glory; lab and all.

He'd put his contingency plan into motion. All he had to do was sit back and wait. Within a year the entire population of the world would be gone and he could start running things his way. Thank God he hadn't taken the injection himself.

⟋⟍

The conversation with Steve had left John feeling ill at ease. He'd never been a close friend, but he'd hadn't been antagonistic before. The idea of the complex being bugged made him uncomfortable. They were only a research facility.

His gut instinct told him something was going on but he couldn't figure out what it was. He'd have to keep his eyes open.

John went to his desk to get his notes. Rummaging through the remnants of vending machine meals, he found them.

"Dr. Conners?" a soft voice called. "I'm sorry to bother you, but would you take a look at these printouts?" Coming towards him was his senior assistant, Kara Collins. John couldn't help admiring her long, shapely legs.

He looked down at the clipboard Kara held out to him. Across the paper she'd written, "Go to the parking lot now! Say aloud that you left your keys in your car. I'll meet you there!"

With a puzzled look John said, "I see the problem. Let me show you." Taking the pencil he wrote, "O.K."

"Thank you Dr. Conners," Kara said with a nervous smile. "That makes more sense! By the way; I'm leaving early. I'm not feeling well. I hope it won't be a problem."

"If you're sick, you belong in bed not here slaving over a hot computer," John said with an artless attempt at humor. "Go home and rest."

Crushing the paper, Kara slipped it into her pocket. "Thanks Doc."

It looked like his instinct was right, but how was Kara involved? John brushed his shaggy brown hair out of his eyes and walked to his desk. Hunting around in his pockets he exclaimed, "I left my keys in the car again!" With a sigh of frustration he left the lab and headed for the parking lot.

Kara was standing beside a sporty red convertible with the door open. "Get in!"

"Don't you think this is a strange way to get a date?" John asked.

"If you want to stay alive, get in the car!" Kara ordered.

For the first time John noticed how pale she was. "Okay, but you have some explaining to do."

Kara drove towards the guardhouse. "Buckle your seatbelt; if there's any trouble I'm going through the gate."

John looked at her with wide-eyed astonishment but did as she said. The guard didn't look up as he opened the gate.

Kara pulled onto the road and let out a loud sigh of relief. "We need to talk and we don't have much time."

A block up the road, Kara pulled into the bank parking lot. "We need to empty our accounts," Kara said.

Before she could jump out of the car, John grabbed her arm. "You expect me to do this without an explanation? I have to get those autopsies done! Please take me back to the lab."

Sitting back in the seat John crossed his arms over his chest and waited to see how far Kara was going to carry this practical joke.

"John please!" Kara pleaded. "I overheard Mr. King talking to Eileen. After you leave today somebody will be bringing computers into the lab and taking the old ones. He said you wouldn't be back. Craig is supposed to clear out your desk and take everything to Mr. King.

"After I heard that I had an idea. I know what time the security guard goes outside for a cigarette so I snuck into the security office while he was gone and played back the video from Mr. King's office this morning."

Kara told John about the phone calls Mr. King made. "Now would you please go with me and get whatever money you have? We need to move fast!"

John climbed out of the car and followed Kara into the bank. He gave himself a pinch hard enough to bruise, and decided that as crazy as all of this sounded, it wasn't a dream.

John went to the teller and withdrew his life savings, Kara did the same. Between them they had $35,000. In a few moments, they were speeding towards John's house.

"How did you know the lab was bugged?" John asked.

"Craig the security guard told me. He said Mr. King used to come to the security booth to spy on the employees."

"Kara, why did you get involved? You weren't in danger before you warned me. You've put your life at risk!"

"I know the results of those autopsies. How long would it take Mr. King to decide that I'm a threat to him too? Besides, when I was born, I wasn't given the ESI."

"That's impossible! The ESI has been used globally for twenty years."

"Not everywhere it hasn't. My parents were botanists. They were in the jungles of South America when my mother gave birth to me."

The full impact of what he'd done hit John and he was overcome with sickening waves of nausea. "I'm responsible for the extermination of the entire human race," he said in a horrified voice.

"Like hell you are. I heard you tell Mr. King that you wanted to do further testing. We don't have time for you to sit around and play martyr. We'd better figure out a solution, fast!"

Giving himself a mental shake, John agreed. "I know a good place to hide, the lab where I discovered the ESI. When we got government grants Steve moved us to a new lab. As far as I know, he locked the door and never went back. Everything should still be there."

Kara parked in front of Johns' house. She looked around to make sure they hadn't been followed. "Looks like the coast is clear."

She took a close look at his house and was astounded. It was a huge, sprawling monstrosity. Tree limbs seemed to hover protectively over the badly shingled roof. Weeds had choked out the once beautiful flower beds and the hedges were in desperate need of trimming.

Mistaking her gasp of astonishment for admiration, John said, "Isn't it a beauty? I inherited it from my parents."

"You're kidding, right?" Kara asked.

"You need the eye of an artist and the soul of a poet to see its beauty. You're too artistically stunted." John snickered.

Kara stepped out of the car and walked across the uneven bricks to the weather-beaten front door.

"Welcome to my castle!" John said unlocking the door and ushering her inside.

While John packed what he needed, Kara looked around.

"Who would ever believe such beauty was hidden inside?" she thought.

The delicate crystal chandeliers kissed every surface they touched with sparkling raindrops of prismatic colors. The hardwood floors were warmed with a golden glow and every wooden surface was a silken mirror.

Settling into a chair Kara thought, "The eye of an artist, and the soul of a poet; how right he was."

"I think we'll be safer buying supplies at a store. I don't want to spend to much time here," John said as he came into the living room carrying three large suitcases.

"I thought men always packed light!" Kara said with a mischievous smile.

"Hey, I need my CD player, Mickey Mouse night light, you know, all the comforts of home," he said with a smile. "Let's load this stuff into my van, it's parked in the garage." They carried the cases out to the midnight blue minivan.

They agreed it would be best for John to follow Kara instead of leaving her car in front of his house.

Kara's house was the exact opposite of John's. Everything

was modern and airy. Wildflowers and plants were everywhere.

It didn't take Kara long to get her things together. She had three large cases too, John noted with amusement. "Necessities," she said with a grin as she noticed John eyeing her bags. They quickly loaded her possessions into the van and pulled out into the street.

"I've been thinking," Kara said. "There's a Bi-Lo Market just over the county line. We'll blend into a large crowd and there's a chance that nobody will remember us later."

Shopping turned out to be a pleasant surprise for both of them. They both liked fresh fruits and vegetables, and both loved spaghetti and meatballs. They stopped in front of an Oreo cookie display. Grinning like children they put two packages apiece into the cart.

"I usually put off grocery shopping until there's nothing left in my cupboards but spider webs," John admitted with an embarrassed smile.

"I'm the same way," Kara said, blue eyes dancing. "I'd rather eat food out of vending machines."

"Vending machine food? Nobody eats that stuff! They put road kill, crushed up cockroaches...."

"Stop or I'm going to puke all over your loafers," Kara interrupted looking slightly green.

"Sorry," John said as they picked up their bags and hurried to the van.

After putting the last bag in the van, John turned to Kara. "I don't know if there's anything we can do to make things right, but I'm glad you're here with me."

John hugged Kara, inhaling the soft scent of Enjoli perfume clinging to her silky blonde hair.

"Come on," she said backing away. "Mankind's waiting for us to pull a miracle out of thin air. We'd better get started."

The van bounced its way up the rutted, overgrown dirt road.

John gritted his teeth and clenched the steering wheel. "It looks like this place has been forgotten."

He drove around the back of the lab. "I'm going to open the door; you pull the van in, okay?"

With a quick nod of assent, Kara unbuckled her seat belt and slid over to the driver's seat.

Squealing loudly, the doors opened and Kara drove the van inside.

"Get those flashlights out of that box behind my seat, would you?" John asked. "We're going to have to turn the power back on."

After getting the power on, they made several trips to the van to get their supplies. They put everything in the staff living quarters.

"Nobody wasted money *here*," Kara thought as she surveyed the Spartan surroundings.

"I've got to get into the computers at the new complex and copy my files," John said as he sat down at the computer and began to type. "I hope they haven't taken the computers out yet."

After several minutes John sighed with relief. "They haven't gotten into my files, I just downloaded them. They're printing out."

While they waited for the files to print, John and Kara ate roast beef sandwiches and drank Diet Pepsi.

"Ironic isn't it?" Kara asked with a smile "The world is coming to an end, and we're still counting calories." She gestured toward the cans she was putting into a recycle bin.

"The irony is that you recycled the cans," John said laughing with her.

"As soon as those files are done printing, I want to check a couple of things. While I'm doing that, could you do me a favor? There's supposed to be a secret government lab that was set up to breed genetically superior test-tube babies. When the population dwindled they were supposed to start breeding smarter, healthier specimens of humanity. The government should have a file of parents. I want to know where the lab is and if they've started breeding yet. If they have, I want a list of the parents."

The computer spit out its last piece of paper and fell silent. "Let's get to work."

After several hours Kara stretched and turned to John. "I've got bad news. There's no trace of a facility set up for test-tube babies, and I can't locate a list of parents. Either it hasn't been set up yet it's a well-kept secret."

Yawning widely Kara said, "Let's call it a day. I'm too tired to concentrate. We'll start fresh in the morning." Turning off the computer monitors, they went to their adjoining rooms. Neither one of them slept well.

The next morning while John sipped coffee and read files, Kara wandered into the kitchenette. John took one look at Kara and sprayed coffee all over the table. "What in the world are you wearing?" he asked in between bouts of laughter.

"My pajamas of course!" Kara answered indignantly. "What, you have something against bunny p.j.'s?"

"I could probably ignore the pajamas, but those huge pink slippers that look like rabbits feet kill me!"

"Well at least my feet only *look* big!" Kara said as she looked down at John's scuffed loafers pointedly.

"I'm sorry. I've never seen anything like those slippers before!"

"No more cracks about my wardrobe, buddy."

Just then John heard his name on the radio. "Authorities are looking for Dr. Conners in connection with the theft of classified information from King Labs, Inc. Anyone with any information on his whereabouts is asked to contact the authorities immediately."

"Well, that didn't take long," Kara said. "I wonder why they didn't include me? I'm sure the guard remembers us leaving together yesterday."

"I don't know," John replied. "It doesn't make any sense."

"Craig isn't going to tell Mr. King he showed me the video monitors," Kara said thoughtfully. "They don't have any idea what you know. All they know is neither of us has shown up for work today."

"Remember, you told me you weren't feeling well yesterday and that you were leaving early? That has to be on tape," John said. "They may think I bummed a ride from you. If that's the case, it could work in our favor."

"Last night as I was falling asleep I realized something. We need one of the Capuchins. I can't do any research without tissue cultures. I'd like to verify my results to make sure there aren't any mistakes. Ready to go into the lions den?"

"No!" Kara said forcefully.

"It's the only way, Kara. Maybe the security guard wasn't

paying attention when we left yesterday and that's why they're not looking for you," John said as he got up to get another cup of coffee.

"I'd better get dressed," Kara said. "I'll drive your van to the parking garage about a block from my house, then pick up my car."

"If I'm not back by 7 p.m. you'll know it was a trap and you'll have to think of something else." Kara set her cup on the counter and walked into her room.

John looked up from his monitor as Kara came back dressed in a soft green sweater and black dress pants.

"If the guard looks the least bit suspicious don't go in! Just turn around and get out of there," John said worriedly.

"Don't worry, I'll be careful. By the way, you're cooking tonight. I like pasta and lots of salad," Kara said as she headed out the door.

John turned to his monitor. He'd found his old research data on the ESI. He started running computer simulations on the chemical make-up. He wanted to see what was altering the genes and causing the premature aging. Several hours later, John was stiff from sitting so long and decided he needed a break.

As he finished eating a bologna sandwich he heard the computer signaling that it was done running its program.

He hurried over to look at the DNA simulation on the screen. After studying the screen for several moments, he sank into his chair. There was no way to stop the premature aging.

Kara pulled up to the guardhouse at King Labs. "Running a little late this morning Ms. Collins?"

"Yes, I had to change a flat."

"Well it's a good thing you knew how!" the old guard said as he pushed the button to open the gate.

Kara drove onto the lot and parked. Wiping her sweaty palms against her pants, she entered the building. As she slid her key card into the slot by her office she heard a voice behind her.

"Good morning Ms. Collins. I assume there's a reason for your tardiness," Mr. King said.

Kara turned to face him and told him the same story she'd told the guard.

"I don't suppose you know where Dr. Conners is this morning?"

"No. I haven't seen him since yesterday. I left work early. I wasn't feeling well and Dr. Conners asked for a lift into town. He said there was something wrong with his car. Somebody was supposed to tow it to a garage for him."

"His car's still in his space and the guard at the gate couldn't remember him leaving yesterday," said Mr. King. "I wanted to speak to both of you this morning. A virus attacked our computer system last night. I had new computers installed but I'm afraid you're going to have to start from scratch."

"This will set our research back indefinitely!" Kara fumed. "Don't we have master discs?"

"Of course we have a set of master discs, but it seems they've been misplaced. You get started and I'll see if I can locate Dr. Conners." As he opened the door, Mr. King stopped and turned back to Kara. "By the way, where did you drop Dr. Conners at yesterday?"

"Out at the Airport Restaurant, he said he was meeting a friend for dinner." There, she thought, that'll give him something to worry about!

"Did you happen to notice if he was carrying a briefcase with him?"

"Yes, he went to his car and got an overnight case. He said it was personal things he didn't want to leave in the car while it was in the garage."

"Well I guess that'll be all then," Mr. King said as he turned and left the room.

࿐

Kara was stooped down trying to lift a box of files that was spilling all over the floor when two darkly tanned hands reached down and picked up the box for her. "Looks like you could use some help," a deep voice said close to her ear.

Looking up, Kara saw a dark-haired man with arresting green eyes. "Sure, follow me."

As they went into the office she said, "You can set that down anywhere. I'm Kara Collins, Senior Research Assistant. Although right now I'm more of a glorified file clerk," she said with a rueful laugh.

"I'm Aaron King. I guess my title would be boss's son," he

said as he eyed her appreciatively.

Well, there goes his Prince Charming image, Kara thought sourly to herself. Aloud she said, "Please excuse me, I've got a lot to do."

"No problem, see ya around honey," Aaron said sauntering out the door.

After making sure nobody was in the hallway, Kara headed for the animal lab.

Walking across the room she looked for video cameras but didn't see any. Next she checked the door on the loading dock and found it unlocked.

Kara walked out the back door, got in her car and drove it around to the loading dock. She ran back to check the hall and hurried to the freezer.

Grimacing at the feel of the hard little body inside the plastic bag; she raced out the door and put it in her trunk

Kara drove quickly to the gate. "I'm going to get some lunch," she told the guard, "can I pick anything up for you?"

"No thanks, my wife always packs my lunch. She wants to keep an eye on my cholesterol."

Once she was through the gate, Kara floored the accelerator. She sped to the parking garage where she'd left John's van. Parking her car, she transferred the monkey into the van. With a sigh of relief, she headed for the lab.

Kara walked into the living quarters and laid the frozen carcass on the table. "I'm never going back there again! I was scared to death I'd get caught."

John walked over, put his arms around Kara and said, "I ran the DNA projections on the computer while you were gone. It's telling me there's no way to undo the damage once you've been injected."

"There has to be something the computer's missing. You're still going to take the tissue samples and check again aren't you?"

"Of course I am, but for now I'm going to take our friend and put him in the freezer. Then you and I are going to sit down to the spaghetti dinner I cooked and you can tell me about your day. Why don't you grab a shower while I take care of things here?"

"That sounds like a lovely idea."

John put the monkey in the freezer, came back to the kitchen and furiously scrubbed his hands. He set a large mixing bowl of salad at Karas' place. "She did say she likes lots of salad," he chuckled. He put a bowl of spaghetti and meatballs, a loaf of garlic bread and a small bowl of fresh fruit on the table.

Just as he finished, Kara came into the kitchen. Her skin was flushed from the heat of the water and her hair clung in small, damp ringlets to her fragrant skin.

The large bowl of salad sitting in front of one of the places at the table made her burst into laughter. "I bet I know who sits here," she said sliding into her chair.

"You did specify lots of salad," John said smiling. He sat down in the chair across from Kara and helped himself to the spaghetti. "So tell me what happened today."

Kara gave him a rundown on everything that had happened at the lab. "I just hope I didn't overplay it. I was trying to give him a red herring to follow at the airport. It might buy us a little more time."

"You're sure you weren't followed?" he asked nervously. "I don't like the idea of Aaron turning up now."

"As far as I could tell, no."

"I'd feel safer if the security system was armed," John said as he left the table.

By the time he came back Kara had cleared the table and washed the dishes. "Are you going to do the cultures tonight?" she asked.

"There's no sense waiting until tomorrow. If the computer simulation is right, we need to start working on alternatives."

⚕

Just as Kara started to doze off, John came into the living room. "The computer is right, there's no way to reverse the aging process." He sat down on the couch beside her. Taking Kara's hand in his, he turned his troubled face towards her. "There's no way to undo the damage I've caused."

Kara pulled him against her and stroked his hair. "It's not your fault." Smoothing his hair back from his face, she kissed his forehead.

John's arms encircled Kara. "I think I'd go crazy if I had to go through this alone."

Slowly he brought his lips down to meet hers. "If you don't want this to go any further," John whispered huskily, "now's the time to say so." Kara's only answer was to pull him close.

The next morning Kara smiled as John came into the kitchen. "You look like you had a rough night. Have a cup of coffee while I fix breakfast."

John sat at the table and sipped coffee. "I think we ought to go public."

"We'll cause a panic if we do that," Kara said as she sat down beside him.

"We need to take this information to the media for two very good reasons," John explained patiently. "The most important reason is that Mr. King won't come after us once everyone knows what's going on, he'll be to busy covering his butt.

"The second reason is that it's only right for people to have a chance to prepare themselves. You need to fax a copy of these files to every worldwide news agency, Kara."

"What are you going to be doing while I'm doing that?"

"I'm going to be incinerating the carcass of our friend. When I've finished that I'm going to look around and see if we have everything we need to set up our own nursery. You're going to be the mother of our next generation."

"How am I going to accomplish that?" Kara squeaked. "How many babies are we talking about? How am I supposed to care for them? Where am I supposed to care for them?"

"Slow down a minute. I'm going to be around to help you, for awhile. We can buy a ranch out in the country where you'll be safe from the riots. Kara, we can do this if we take it one step at a time."

"I don't know if I can do this, John! Please, hold me for a minute, okay?"

"You'd better get started, it's going to take awhile to fax all of this stuff," John said as he pulled away from Kara.

"Okay," she said as she gathered up the files and sat down at the fax machine. An hour later, Kara turned to John. "Have you heard anything yet?"

"Nothing. I wonder what's going on. I've been surfing the channels but there hasn't been anything. The government must've found a way to keep the media from putting this on the air. In the interest of public safety of course," he added sarcastically.

"Then we're still in danger?" Kara asked.

"I'm afraid so. Our only hope is to go public."

"Wait!" Kara reached over and turned up the TV.

"Yes, I've heard this rumor but I assure you there's no truth to it. People aren't going to start falling dead in the streets! Scientists found a flaw in the process but they assure me it's not fatal. Until we have more information, I urge the American people to stay calm." Ignoring the uproar around him, the President turned and left the podium.

"That's it then," John said helplessly. "They're going to whitewash it."

As they started to stack the folders on the desk, John remembered he hadn't turned the security system on after going out to the incinerator.

"I'll take care of it," Kara said. "I need a breath of fresh air anyway."

After Kara left, John picked up the inventory list and started reading through it again. There were a lot of things they could utilize for their nursery. Frowning in concentration he added a few more items to the list.

After awhile John realized that Kara had been gone a long time.

He went to his room to get his pistol and the extra clip he carried in the glove compartment of the van. When they'd taken up residence here, he'd felt safer with it close at hand.

'John entered the garage and looked around. What he saw rooted him to the floor. Standing by the van was Aaron King, one arm wrapped tightly around Karas' waist, the other holding a wicked looking knife to her throat. Her enormous blue eyes begged for help.

"It's about time you got here! I was beginning to think I'd have to come looking for you." Without any warning Aaron pulled the knife across Kara's throat, dropping her blood-gushing corpse to the ground.

"No!" John screamed. Bringing the gun up he emptied it at Aaron.

"That's what I like about amateurs!" Aaron called as he

ducked behind the van. "You can always count on them to do something unexpected." Aaron pulled his handkerchief from his breast pocket and wound it tightly around his arm where one of the bullets had grazed him.

John dodged behind a stack of tires and slammed the extra clip into his gun. "I'm going to kill you, Aaron!"

"Not in this lifetime, pencil pusher."

Sliding around the front of the van, Aaron came face to face with John.

"Wait! I've got some information you'd like to have. My Dad set up a lab for test-tube babies, did you know that?"

"You have one minute to say your prayers. That's more than you gave Kara and a lot more than you deserve."

Aaron saw the cold determination in John's face. "He's already bred a dozen kids; they're five years old. He has a bunch of scientists raising them."

"So they'll be his legacy. He has the same amount of time left that I do — very little. Thirty seconds."

"No, he never took the injection! He set up a lab after the ESI went on the market and had some scientists finish the research he wouldn't let you complete. He's known about the flaw for five years. When they brought their findings to him, he called a meeting at the lab.

"Dad didn't show up, I did. I blew the place sky high," Aaron bragged. "Anybody who knew anything was killed in that explosion."

"Tell me where the test-tube babies are!" John demanded.

"So you can put a bullet in me as soon as I do? Make me a deal; my life for the location for the lab."

"Your life... for now. I'll come looking for you as soon as I take care of your father."

Aaron started edging back around the van. When he reached the back bumper he smiled at John. "You know I'll be waiting for you don't you?"

"I hope so. It'll save me the trouble of hunting you down."

"The lab's about a mile up the lake from Dad's cabin. Just follow the deer trail. There's no security system. Dad didn't figure anybody'd find out about the lab." Without warning Aaron bolted out the door.

John walked over to Kara, knelt down and pulled her into his arms.

They'd just begun to care for each other and he'd lost her. Holding her tightly he cried for her, for himself, for the future they could've built together. Lowering her to the floor he went to look for a shovel.

⤳⟿

John knelt by her grave. "I promise I'll get those kids! They'll be raised to understand what humans should be!" John turned and stumbled back to the garage.

⤳⟿

Aaron drove toward the lab where his father was waiting. Daddy wasn't going to be pleased. Not only had he failed to kill John Conners; but he'd given him directions to the lab!

His father was talking on the phone when Aaron entered the office. Hanging up the phone, Steve motioned him to a chair. "Well, did you take care of them?"

"Not exactly," Aaron answered. He stalked to the bar and helped himself to a bottle of water. "The girl's dead, but Dr. Conners is coming here. Don't worry, I'll take care of him."

"What were you thinking? The President has flown in scientists from around the world to start mass production of test-tube babies. Every government has donated sperm and eggs with the agreement that we'll re-populate their countries as well as our own. Those fools don't realize that with all their scientists here, I can pick and choose who gets babies and who doesn't. Just think of the power I have!"

And John called *me* psychotic, Aaron thought to himself in amazement. He's holding the entire world hostage! If this place goes, so does the future. There won't be anyone left with enough knowledge to do what's being done here. In one year the human race will be extinct.

"Get out there and get rid of him this time!" Steve ordered. "I've got government troops being flown in to guard the lab but until they get here we can't take any chances."

Aaron hummed softly to himself as he went out the door. He walked to the trunk of his car and started rummaging around in some cardboard boxes.

John hid his car in an overgrown orchard and walked along

the deer trail. He picked his way through the tangled vines until he could see the outline of the lab against the sky. Staying low to the ground he scurried through the grass and slid down against a tree trunk. From here he could watch the lab.

He hadn't believed a word Aaron said about the security system. Only a fool would walk in the front door.

He watched as people entered and left the building. People were coming out to have a cigarette then going back inside. As far as he could tell, there weren't any security checks at the door.

Standing up, he circled around to the side of the building where people sat at an old picnic table. Acting as if he were butting out a cigarette he'd picked up off the ground unnoticed, John strolled to the door and walked in.

Just to the right of the door was a sign. "All employees are to maintain a sterile field at all times! Please use showers and change into greens before entering the lab. Thank You." Beside the sign was a door marked "Showers".

I couldn't have planned this better if I'd tried, John thought to himself. He hurried into the room, grabbed a set of clothes, and entered a cubicle. After changing and stuffing his clothes into an empty locker, he peeked around the curtain to watch the people coming in and out. Nobody was wearing a security ID badge.

Carefully he pushed the pistol down the front of his pants and pulled his shirt over it. He checked the mirror at the back of the cubicle to see if there was a tell-tale bulge. Screwing up his courage, he followed a group of people into the elevator.

John listened to the conversations around him. He found out the offices were on the top floor, and the incubators were in the basement.

As he started towards the front of the elevator to get off, the door opened and Aaron stepped in carrying a heavy looking briefcase. John moved as far back in the car as he could, turned his head so his face was partially hidden and prayed Aaron wouldn't see him.

Aaron seemed preoccupied and rode to the basement without bothering to look around. After he got off, John breathed a quiet sigh of relief.

Getting off on the top floor, John strode down the hall to

the door with Steve King's name on it. He pushed it open and stepped inside.

A startled secretary looked up. "May I help you sir?" she asked.

"Is Mr. King in?"

"No, he stepped out a little while ago. Is there anything I can help you with?"

"No, thanks, I'll see if I can find him myself."

John decided not to risk running into Aaron on the elevator again and headed for the stairs. He clambered down the steps and opened the door to the basement.

Standing with his back toward him, talking to someone in a lab coat was Steve King.

John walked over, slipped his arm around Steve's shoulder and pushed the barrel of the pistol into his ribs.

"Steve! You're just the man I'm looking for! Is there somewhere we can talk? I've got something you're going to get the biggest bang out of!"

"Sure John, follow me." They turned and walked to a set of double-doors a little further down the hallway. "We can talk in here."

The moment they were through the doors, Steve turned on John. "How dare you pull a gun on me!"

"Not another word or I'll kill you where you stand," John said.

Looking around, he saw an alcove with a couple of chairs. John pulled Steve toward him. "We're going to sit down and talk, or we can do it the easy way and I'll kill you now. What do you say?"

With mounting fear, Steve realized these next few moments could be his last. "All right John, let's talk," he said as he walked on rubbery legs to one of the chairs and collapsed onto it.

John sat on the chair next to Steve and pushed the gun into his ribcage. "Do I have to tell you not to do anything foolish?"

"No, just tell me what you think you're doing! We've been friends for a long time and...."

"Cut the crap, Steve. I know about the video cameras at the lab, I know about the lab full of scientists you had Aaron murder, and I know you sent your psycho son to kill Kara and I. I know in about a year I'm going to die of old age and you're not. How much more do I need to know before I decide you should be exterminated, you lousy excuse for a human being?"

"Hold on a minute, you weren't injected either! I told the doctor to substitute water."

John's mouth dropped open in shock. "Why did you do that?"

"Your research wasn't complete; I didn't want to take any chances. If there was something wrong, who better to find a solution than the genius that invented it? Five years ago my scientists found a flaw. That's when I hoped you'd find it too."

"How did you think you were going to keep me from telling the world about this?" John asked angrily.

"That's easy. I know you. You'd never tell the world it was dying unless you had a way to save it. Guilt would've eaten at you like a cancer until you had a cure. You're too predictable."

"You still haven't told me why you wanted a cure."

"After you found the cure and I got rid of you, nobody else would know. I could choose the people I wanted, cure them, and let the rest rot in hell. Mankind doesn't mean squat to me. Power! That means everything!"

"Hello again!" a voice said from behind John. "Take that nasty little peashooter out of Daddy's ribs and hand it to me."

John took the gun from Steve's side and held it out to Aaron. "Now what?"

Aaron wrenched the gun from his hand. Pointing his gun at them, Aaron said, "This way if you please gentlemen. We're going to Daddy's favorite room."

They walked down the hall and stopped in front of a gray metal door. Steve reached into his pocket, extracted a keyring, and unlocked the door.

There was no need to turn on a light. The brightness of video monitors lit up the room. All three of the men entered. "Lock it and give me the keys!" Aaron told his father.

Aaron walked to a console. "This evening for your viewing pleasure, we have a special treat." Keeping an eye on the two men he rapidly pushed a series of buttons. All of the monitors showed different rooms in the building.

John gasped in horror. There was enough plastic explosives

in the lab to blow them all to kingdom come.

"Please Aaron, think about what you're doing!" John begged.

"Oh, but I have. My father's always been a great believer in power." Holding a remote control detonator aloft he continued, "But this; this is real power! I have the power to destroy the entire world."

Howling like a madman, Steve launched himself at his son. As they grappled on the floor the detonator flew out of Aaron's grasp and landed beneath the control console.

The keys flew across the room and clattered to a stop at John's feet. Snatching them up, he ran for the door. As the key turned in the lock, he heard a dull thump behind him. Like Lot's wife, he had to turn and see the destruction that lay behind him. Steve was sprawled on the floor in a spreading pool of his own blood.

"Go ahead, run!" Aaron yelled. "It's going to take me at least a minute to get that detonator out from under there." Aaron scrambled to his knees holding the gun on John with one hand and searching for the detonator with the other.

John ran. He knew there wasn't a snowball's chance in hell of getting out of here alive or of warning anyone else, but he ran anyway. Scorching, orange light enveloped him as he ran for the stairs.

⟨⟩

June 25, 2005

The children chased butterflies and splashed in the creek as the small group of adults sat back and watched them.

"I can't believe it's been five years already," John said.

"I know," agreed Cheryl. "When we pulled you from the wreckage, I didn't think you were going to make it."

"Tell me about it," John said. "I thought I'd died and gone to heaven — until the pain kicked in anyway."

"How sweet! You thought I was an angel," Cheryl said, patting her golden hair and showing her dimples.

"Spare me," said an older man sitting beside her. "It was my beard and innocent face he saw."

"Knock it off you guys!" John laughed. "I really do believe it was a miracle that someone like Steve had the foresight to keep some people from getting the injection so they could be caregivers for the kids, just in case something went wrong."

"No, the real miracle was that we decided on the spur of the moment to take the kids for a walk that day," Cheryl said.

Just then a dark, curly haired little girl ran over and climbed into John's lap. "Papa, can I please go in the creek too? Adam said only boys were allowed," she pouted.

"Adam!" John shouted to the husky boy splashing happily. "Eve and the other girls are allowed in the creek too! Remember, we're all equal. That's the rule!"

Giggling happily, Eve jumped down and ran to the creek with several other little girls.

"John, have you noticed even though these kids were bred with super intelligence, they still act like any other kid you've ever seen?" Cheryl asked.

"Yeah," John said smiling happily from his wheelchair. "We've done a great job of raising them haven't we? I had a friend that believed in our future and these kids. I think she'd be happy with what we've accomplished."

Slowly John rolled his wheelchair closer to the creek. "I miss you Kara, I wish you were here. Our future is looking brighter than it ever has before. I kept my promise, Kara. I kept my promise."

Kenra J. Miller

I am a 45-year-old grandmother of three. I've been raising my 5- and 6-year-old grandsons for the past five years, which hasn't left much time for writing — believe me!

I have written a lot of children's stories but "World Without End" is my first adult story. The idea for this story came from a news report about women in India being sterilized.

I'd like to dedicate this story to my children. I've always told them, "You can do anything you want to do if you're willing to take a chance and work for it!"

I also want to thank my cousin John. He game me an old Packard Bell computer, read the first draft of this story, and told me, "I believe in you." Thanks, John.

A Rhesus to Believe
Greg Stoker

Monday morning at 8:03. Oh, yeah. This is my favorite time to visit the boss, Eric thought to himself. He sat in the office waiting for Mr. Lechner to appear. Judy, a forty year veteran of the company, answered the phone as the executive assistant when it rang and ignored Eric when it didn't.

Eric stood up to get himself a cup of coffee when Bruce Lechner entered into the office looking disheveled.

"Eric," he said with a little enthusiasm. His voice was weary. "Come in."

The two men entered and closed the door. Eric sat down and waited for Lechner to finish shuffling papers from a portfolio.

"Eric, I know you are going to have some problems with this but it is going to happen." As usual, Lechner delivered the order with full eye contact and kept it there during the rest of the conversation. "We will be working with another lab on part of our research."

"Which part?" Eric was quick to ask.

"Non-Nucleoside RT inhibitors."

Alarm bells went off in the back of Eric's mind. "Don't tell me we are bringing in animals for testing."

"Eric, this is going to happen." Lechner remained firm without breaking his concentration. "A Rhesus monkey to be exact. If you have a problem with this —"

Eric took a deep breath and leaned forward. "You know I'm not much of an activist, Bruce. I just don't want my staff and I to become zoo keepers. Animal research isn't the best way anymore."

"Working with this other lab will help us get around one of the problems. Time has always been a factor. No longer." There was a bit of hesitancy for Lechner to continue. It was rare to see this in the man. "We will be working with ourselves a year in the future."

Eric did not respond. Instead, he sat back and gave Lechner a look that was probably the most incredulous he had seen in his life. He seriously doubted the sanity of his boss for a moment.

"Eric, don't say anything. If you don't believe this then go along with it and cash your paycheck. If what happens doesn't convince you then I won't argue with you."

A smile came to Eric slowly. "You have my interest, boss."

⤢⤡

Eric had a staff of eight researchers and technicians. During a normal day, they were spread out over three offices and two labs plus a break room. Today, they were all huddled into one of the labs when Lechner entered. He was accompanied by a tech from another lab who was carrying a box large enough to hold a Rhesus.

"Not much noise inside here," Eric said while handed the enclosed cage. "Are you sure there is a Rhesus in here?" he said half jokingly.

"I can't verify anything," the tech said, taking the moment too seriously. "My instructions were to bring it here sealed. Opening it is your responsibility, though I am required to watch it."

Eric gave a questioning look to Lechner.

"Take the honors, Eric," Lechner smiled.

Eric placed the container on a lab bench and slid the panel open. Everyone crowded, peering over Eric's shoulder. They saw a baby Rhesus cowering inside, looking at them in fear. Taped to the inside cage was a set of instructions in a plastic bag. He opened them and read the summary out loud.

"Test subject: Mac. Removal of blood samples for *in vitro* culture (included)."

"Ah, he's cute," someone said.

⤢⤡

The routine would never become normal. Each time Mac would arrive from a year in the future, it felt like it was the first time they had met the test subject. They had no memory of previous meetings or experiments. Their only knowledge was the set of instructions to complete in their present time. They had no way of knowing that the first time they had seen Mac was when he was only two months old or that they have seem him a dozen times since then. This was a result of each layer of time overlapping on itself.

Lechner and the same technician walked into the room with Mac for the first time — again.

Eric took the cage and placed it on the lab counter. "OK, let's be careful. This is a noisy one." Squawks and squeals burst forth. When the panel was slid down, the noise abated.

"This is an adult," someone said.

"I was expecting a juvenile," another added.

Eric grabbed the set of instructions and noticed Mac holding a book. He tried to grab it but Mac yelled and screamed until Eric gave up his effort.

"What is it?"

"It's a dictionary," Eric said, puzzled. He opened up the instructions and read them out loud. "Test subject: Mac. Perform fusion/binding inhibitors for cerebellum — *in vivo*."

Unseen, Mac opened the dictionary and looked up *'in vivo'*. When he ran his fingers across the definition, he jumped out of the box. By the time everyone had noticed, he was trying to climb out of a window.

↗↘

The cage was huge this time. The technician had to roll it in on a cart. There was no noise inside but there was a heavy sound when it was set to rest on the floor. As Eric slid the large panel open, the first thing he noticed was the interior lined with plush foam padding under green leather, tuck and rolled. The second item he noticed was an old, gray-haired Rhesus holding a set of instructions and smoking a cigar.

Mac lumbered out of the box on arthritic joints and held the instructions in the air. "All right, listen up people. This is how we're going to do it this time." He handed the set of instructions to Eric who was as dumbfounded as the rest of his staff. "You can read these if you like but I'll tell you right now, I wrote 'em."

Everyone was frozen into place, staring at this hunched over Rhesus giving orders. "Come on, people. Let's snap to it. If we do it right this time, this will be the last time I have to go through this."

Eric stepped forward. "Introductions might be a good way to start," he suggested.

Mac pulled the cigar out. "You're right. I keep forgetting you don't know me. I'm Mac, short for Macaque." His grin showed a wide array of yellow teeth as his two large lips parted.

Eric didn't know what to do. He shuffled his glance around the room. "These people here are —"

"I know who these people are," Mac said. "Sorry, but I have never had patience." He climbed onto a stool and sat on the bench top, pointing around the room. "We have Mary who lives with her two children. Rob is raising a son as a single parent. Steve is single. Kathy is just out of Stanford. Ellen teaches a night class at the local college. Theresa got married last year. Lou has two grandchildren. And Eric — " He paused, lowered his hand, and looked Eric in the face. "Eric has a very good year ahead of him both in and out of the office."

༄༅

Two months later, Lisa starting working as Mac's assistant and within two more months, she and Eric were married. They went on a two-week honeymoon in Mexico during the hottest part of the year but they had found ways to stay near the air conditioner. Eric still returned with a massive sunburn.

His first Monday morning back, they found Mac sitting at his desk they had moved into Eric's office for him. Mac peered over the rim of his granny glasses that had been custom made for his small face and failing vision. "Welcome back." He flashed a wide-grinned smile that has become his trademark since he arrived.

"I stopped at the lab on the way over here." Eric laughed and sat down to get started on the paperwork. Lisa returned to the front portion of the office suite and her desk. "I counted a dozen of your progeny running around with dictionaries trying to talk to one another. It's like watching a bunch of tourists who can't speak the native language."

"Immigrants," Mac said softly. He looked at Eric with the

pride of a father. "I need to go down there. Would you mind giving me a ride?"

"Nope." Eric leaned his shoulder close to Mac so he could climb up and perch.

Mac painfully climbed aboard and wrapped a long simian arm around Eric's head. His tail curled around the collar and hung down the other side. "Let's go."

☽☾

Four months into the year proved to be a painful hump in the spring. Eric came into the lab with a pained look that spoke loudly enough upon his entrance to silence everyone and stop their work. He came over to Mac. Mac looked into Eric's eyes and saw the question he knew would be coming.

"I just heard about Kathy. Her car was broadsided by a semi on the way to work this morning." A gasp sounded around the room. "She was killed instantly."

"I'm sorry," Mac said sincerely.

Eric lowered his voice but it was still audible for everyone to hear. "Did you know it was going to happen?"

All eyes were on Mac. He did not hesitate. "Yes. Yes, I did."

"I thought you might. You're from the future. You've lived this year over and over since you were born. Why didn't you tell us? She could have taken a different route or stayed home." His voice trailed off.

"I did." His tail hung in the air above and behind his head as he held on to a nearby gas nozzle. "I tried warning her the first year I was able to speak with my new vocal cords. Over the years, she took a different route, stayed home or just didn't believe me. It never made a difference. I don't know why."

Eric didn't respond. Like the rest of the day, no one knew what to say.

☽☾

"You look nervous," Eric noticed.

"I am," Mac said. He was surrounded by his children who were talking and generally having fun in the festive atmosphere of Mac's one-year anniversary of arriving from the future. Human and Rhesus alike chatted with each other on mundane topics ranging from the game of chess to plans for the weekend. A year ago, the scene would have been unbelievable but today, it was in the realm of the ordinary.

"Why are you nervous?"

Mac smiled. "As of an hour ago, I am a free Macaque." A high-pitched sound came from him. It was the sound of laughter. "I am free. No more will I be reliving the same year over and over. Everyone staying the same while I age another year."

"I understand," Eric said.

Mac shook his head. "There is no way you would understand unless you went through it yourself but I appreciate the attempt."

Eric sat down so the two of them could whisper. "I meant understand something else."

Mac looked quizzically. "What do you mean?"

"Who really sent you back in time? It wasn't us. There was no decision for us be made."

"It was you, or your lab in another department. It was the same company is what I'm trying to say." Mac was frustrated trying to explain.

"Maybe at first. But not afterwards. When did it change?" Eric stuck to his firm belief.

Reluctantly, Mac answered. "After I snuck a dictionary back with me. I taught myself how to read and from there — speaking. With the help of your surgical team that is." Mac's grin returned showing his pride.

"Then it was you. You took over the program and changed it to something else. What?"

"The original intent was the study of animal intelligence. Trying to define and understand it. The answer was quite simple. All intelligence needs to grow is cognizance. How many people do you know come across stupid at times because they are simply not aware?"

"Too many," Eric chuckled.

"Once I became aware… I didn't want to lose it or be controlled by someone else and live the life of an animal. I also wanted others to be like me." Mac gestured across the room at his children playing and talking.

"Are you going to tell my little secret?" Mac asked.

Eric thought for a moment but the decision was easy. "I'd say we have accomplished more with you at the helm than a barrel full of humans. I want to see what's next."

The two friends shook hands.

Greg Stoker

Greg has been several things from an assistant athletic director at the high school level to a computer programmer/tech. Now semiretired, he finds himself doing what he loved most before he started thinking about a career: writing. He has several short stories published as well as some artwork. He was also an editor for a local Portland magazine called *Storyshop* which specialized in new and emerging talents.

He still lives in the Pacific Northwest with his wife Gloria and their two children, Amanda and Justin. One day, he plans to finish restoring his 1968 Mustang GT(302 Cleveland 4-barrel with factory fog, tilt and fold-down) and is just about ready to accept help from time-traveling monkeys.

The Waiting Game
Ellen Straw

Lieutenant Pamela Olmstead tried not to yawn as the ship's doctor ran diagnostics on her in the medical chamber. Dr. Hoda Saman had just come from a routine scan of the crew contingent that had been selected to remain in cryosuspension during the journey back to Earth. The First Officer was suspended as well; she'd sustained severe injuries on a planet code-named T-75. The ship's resources were so tight that they couldn't afford to keep her conscious, hooked up to equipment, for the few months it would take to get home. Those among the officers and crew of the *New Hope* that were still active would be rotated into suspension as others were brought out of it to take over their duties.

Having felt increasingly ill ever since her return from the planet's surface a week ago, Olmstead had finally decided to do something about it. Uncomfortably warm, she'd discarded her silver duty jacket, black pullover and shoes in favor of her gray undershirt and pants.

"Well, I'm glad T-75 is habitable," she said, "but it was also hazardous — at least for a few of us. Maybe the First Officer and I should apply for combat pay, huh?"

Saman didn't answer. Instead, she looked from the scanner to her patient and back again, in apparent disbelief.

"What's wrong?" the lieutenant asked, trying not to worry. "It's just an exotic bug that they missed during decontamination — right? I made the mistake of walking through that cloud of dust or pollen or whatever it was, and I must have contracted some kind of airborne virus."

Saman looked up, her expression serious. She fixed her dark eyes on Olmstead, placing a hand on her shoulder. "Pam, I don't mince words, so I'll be straight with you: You're pregnant."

Olmstead didn't speak at first, then giggled. "No, that can't be right, Hoda. Something else must be wrong. Or maybe it's your equipment. I haven't been active since we left Earth, and that was months ago. I haven't been with a man on this ship —"

"I know," Saman interrupted, taking a deep breath before continuing. "However you got pregnant, it wasn't by a man. And it certainly wasn't by normal means."

Olmstead could hardly get her next words out: "What are you telling me?"

"There's no trace of semen or sperm. What you're carrying isn't human."

For a moment, Olmstead thought she might faint. She put one hand to her mouth and gripped the edge of the table with the other. She felt herself break out in a cold sweat, then vague sensations: the doctor's hand stroking her short blonde hair, the image of her off-white lab coat and leggings, the sound of her voice.

"What did you say?" the lieutenant whispered.

"For you to lie down, Pam. I've got to tell Captain Parry about this."

"Why?" Olmstead snapped, her voice still raspy but no longer weak. "He doesn't need anything else to worry about. Just get rid of this goddamn thing. You can tell him later."

"It's not that simple," Saman told her firmly. "I don't know what I'm dealing with here. So far, it doesn't appear to be harming you in any way."

"It's harming me by being inside me," Olmstead snapped. "I never asked for this."

Saman went on. "I compared your current bio-scan with the one I did just before you went planet-side. You weren't pregnant prior to a week ago, but now you're already a few months along. Though I don't know its gestation period, it's growing faster than a human child would. And you've had some nausea and fatigue, but that's nothing different from what would have happened if this fetus were human —"

"What are you trying to do, protect it? *I'm* the one who's been violated. I want it gone."

Saman's expression hardened. "I don't want to risk hurting you by trying to remove something I don't understand. And you know very well that I have to report this." She hit the comm button.

Stunned into silence, all Olmstead could feel now were the goosebumps on her bare arms.

"Christ, Hoda. I have crewmembers to protect, a ship to run, and Earth is full of people waiting for me to find another world to colonize because ours is becoming unlivable. And now you're telling me that the only acceptable one we've found is full of biohazards?"

As high-strung as he was, Captain Jon Parry rarely lashed out at anyone — but it was obvious to Olmstead that the strain and responsibility of this mission had worn on him. Standing next to Saman at the foot of the exam table, he ran his hand through his close-cropped red hair in a familiar gesture of frustration.

The doctor sighed. "I wouldn't go so far as to say that, sir. Only one member of the landing party has been affected, and I can't be certain how it's going to be resolved —"

"Exactly. You can't be certain," Parry said sharply. "As long as that's the case, my ship isn't secure."

"That's right, sir," Olmstead spoke up. "There shouldn't even be a debate. I say, destroy this thing before it kills me. Or anyone else."

Parry fixed his clear blue eyes on the doctor. "The lieutenant should be in the Quarantine wing for now, until you can figure out how to proceed. This alien is an intruder; it's invaded my ship by using one of my crewmembers."

"But you don't know its intentions," Saman pointed out.

"I don't suppose it would be safe to put her in suspension for the next few months."

"Probably not. Too many unknowns."

The captain nodded. "I doubt we could spare the extra power for it. Things are tight as it is." He moved closer to Olmstead. "I don't mean to ignore you, Lieutenant. How are you feeling?"

"I'm holding up, sir, but I want to get this over with."

"Both of you have made good points," Saman broke in, "but I don't have any experience with this new life form, and I don't like the thought of destroying something we've never seen before. I need more time to analyze it."

Olmstead began to object, but Parry cut her off. "Fair enough. But we're not putting this to a vote, and we're not going to talk it to death, either. When I have enough information, I'll make my decision."

Olmstead kept her mouth shut when she saw Parry's hard expression.

"Captain," the doctor said quietly, "I can override your decision for medical reasons."

Parry shook his head. "I may have to disregard that particular regulation."

Saman glared at him. "Then I'll have to log my objections in our records."

"I'll deal with any consequences when we get home," he told her. "One more thing: I want this matter kept confidential. It'll get too complicated if anyone else finds out. As far as the rest of the crew is concerned, Olmstead picked up a highly contagious illness. Understood?"

After the others acknowledged him, Parry turned and strode out of the medical chamber.

"Thanks a lot for pursuing your own agenda, Doc," Olmstead said, sitting up. "I thought physicians were supposed to be their patients' advocates."

"Think whatever you want, Pam, but I'm genuinely concerned for your well-being," said Saman. "That's precisely why I don't want to proceed without more analysis. Frankly, I'm surprised you don't feel the same way, with your expertise being general scientific support —"

"All right, fine. I don't have the energy to fight about it right now. Just give me something for the nausea, and I'll be off to my private little prison."

Less than an hour later, the lieutenant found herself marking time in the seldom used, heavily secured area of the ship known as the Q-Wing.

⊘⊗

For Olmstead, the days became a blur of repeated routines: Being examined and scanned; doing as much administrative work as possible; eating; napping; showering; reading; and anything else she could think of to keep her mind off of what had happened to her.

"How do you feel today?"

The question had become absurd. Olmstead kept her answer short: *"Like a lab specimen, Doc."*

Nighttime was hardest. Sleep often eluded her; and if she nodded off, the nightmares came. Nightmares of giving birth to something horrible and ugly, something utterly alien that would attack her and her shipmates without mercy as soon as it emerged.

After a few nights, Olmstead couldn't keep it bottled up anymore and begged Saman, "Please — you've got to destroy this thing before it destroys us."

"How do you know that?" the doctor replied, with the usual calm demeanor that only made Olmstead more upset.

"Never mind how I know! Just do it."

"You have bad dreams, Pam," Saman said gently. "I've seen you thrashing around in your sleep. It's not based on facts. It's your own fear, your subconscious at work."

"Oh, forget it. I should have known." The lieutenant turned away, trudging back to her bed.

Why don't I just kill myself? Olmstead wondered. *I have that power.* But she couldn't do that, and she knew it. She wasn't willing to sacrifice her own life. Not yet.

"I'll hang on in spite of you," she said to the alien being within her. "I'll make you sorry you ever crossed my path."

⟨⟩

Parry came to see her every day, but Olmstead couldn't decide whether he was genuinely concerned about her or about what might happen to his mission. At the end of her first week in Quarantine, he confronted Saman. "I want more details, Hoda. We're fighting time here, you know."

Olmstead watched from behind the Q-Wing's transparent force field.

"It's humanoid, sir, and it's developing more rapidly than human babies do," Saman replied. "She's showing already; you've seen that. I suspect it may be born as we enter Earth's orbit or just after we land, if we remain on schedule. Olmstead's had some problems, but nothing I haven't seen in pregnant women before."

"Very well. Can you get rid of it?"

The doctor hesitated before answering. "You and the lieutenant want it terminated, Captain; I realize that. And if that's what you decide, I'll do it — if you'll take the responsibility for whatever might happen."

"Like what?"

"I don't *know*," Saman sighed. "It's alien physiology. I won't lie to you: I have a problem with taking its life just because it's alien to us. For all we know, it could be a sentient being —"

"Stop right there," Parry said, putting his hand up. "You speculate too much. None of that matters here. This thing made Olmstead pregnant against her will and without her knowledge or consent. That alone is reason enough to do away with it."

Saman's tone was quiet but harsh. "Whatever you say, Captain."

"You're damn right."

"You can both go to hell!" Olmstead shouted. "And take your regulations and theories with you. This happened to me, and it should be *my* decision. You don't understand anything about it."

Saman gazed at her, saying nothing.

Parry looked as if he were about to snap, then took a deep breath before he spoke. "I'm letting that go by this time, Lieutenant, because of the pressure you're under —"

"Don't patronize me, *sir*."

"Keep pushing me, and you'll regret it. I'm going to give you some time to cool off. I'll be back to see both of you tomorrow."

Don't do me any favors, Olmstead thought, after he left. *Nobody knows how I feel. Nobody can.*

ↀↁ

To her astonishment, after just one more week passed, Olmstead woke from a night filled with dreams more joyful and soothing than she'd thought possible after all those nightmares. In the dreams, Olmstead held the baby, warm and soft, glowing like golden sunlight in her arms. She couldn't see its features, but somehow she knew it was a male. He communicated with her — not in words but in a way she couldn't fully comprehend or articulate, letting her know he would never harm her, that he harbored no ill will towards any of them.

Then, in the shower, she felt the baby move. A pleasant sensation, not painful at all.

The baby.

For a moment, Olmstead didn't even feel the water hitting her skin. It was the first time she'd ever thought of the being within her as a baby. She looked down at her belly and stroked it gently.

"You wouldn't hurt me — would you?" she whispered. "You'd never do that to any of us. For a while, I was afraid you would, but now I think I was wrong."

As soon as she'd gotten dressed, Olmstead hit the comm button on her wall and called Saman.

A short time later, they summoned Parry to the medical chamber, telling him it was urgent.

Parry arrived, and the doctor walked with him to the Q-Wing. Olmstead pointed at the sterile transfer slot on the wall outside her current living space. The mechanism sterilized whatever a quarantined patient had touched before it reached anyone on the outside. Parry picked up the wafer-thin document, written on a clear board, and read it quickly. After a withering look at Saman, he faced Olmstead.

"You're filing a Level One grievance against me?" he said, clenching his fists. "You think I'm jeopardizing your life?"

"You're trying to pressure the doctor to perform a questionable medical procedure on me for very flimsy reasons," Olmstead told him. "At this point, I'm not sure how far you'd go, and that frightens me."

Parry shook his head. "Just a few weeks ago you couldn't wait to be rid of this thing, and suddenly you change your mind?"

"It wasn't sudden —"

"I never thought my own officers would betray me," he interrupted.

"It's not a betrayal, sir," Saman told him. "The situation is too complex for your simple solution."

"You're tying my hands with this. Saman, when did you know about it?"

"Not until a few minutes ago, when Pam asked me to co-sign it."

"I know you've got a lot to deal with, sir," Olmstead said softly. "I'm only trying to protect myself — and the baby. He's not a 'thing.'"

Parry peered at her. "How do you know it's a 'he'?"

"I can't explain that — but I've already named him Alexander."

The captain's tone suddenly changed from one of outrage to unconvincing concern. "Are you feeling all right, Lieutenant?"

"*What?*" Olmstead was taken aback.

"You're not thinking straight. That alien is influencing your thought patterns."

"There's nothing wrong with her mental capacity," Saman said firmly. "Captain, I know what you're doing. You're trying to find a legal way to override Pam's grievance — but you have no proof."

"I can replace you in a second, Doctor," he said.

"Yes, but you don't have sufficient grounds. And my replacement would have to be let in on our little secret. Sir, you don't need to compromise your career over this. Pam's doing fine. Let's just see how it goes."

"I'll stay in the Q-Wing until we get home, Captain," Olmstead spoke up. "No one will be in any danger."

"Right. Until you give birth," Parry retorted. "By then it might be too late. I've been a fool to let it go on *this* long." He paused to rub his eyes before continuing. "We're on the way back to Earth with bad news for everyone: We've found the perfect colony planet, but its life forms will use us as hosts for reproduction; and to top it off, we're infested already."

"Jon, if this alien had wanted to kill us, wouldn't it have done so by now?" Saman inquired.

"How the hell do I know?" he snapped. "All I know is that neither of you has convinced me we're not doomed." The captain turned away abruptly, heading for the door. "This isn't over," he said, just before he slipped out.

"Is it strange that I understand how he feels? How afraid he is?" asked Olmstead.

"Not at all. You had the same feelings."

"Yes, but I was never as xenophobic. This whole thing has

brought that part of him out in force. We can't trust him. I'm scared for the baby."

Unable to touch the other woman through the force field, Saman nevertheless put her hand up, as if to press her palm against Olmstead's. "I know. I won't let anything happen to either of you."

"It's important that Alexander survives. I can't explain it — it's something he communicated to me in a way that no one else can ever understand. Promise me we'll be all right, Hoda."

"I promise."

⚝⚝

The next few weeks were uneventful, yet tense. Parry didn't come around the Medical area much; and when he did, he behaved strangely. He'd invent some reason for showing up, then pace around, sneaking glances at her. One day she overheard him ask Saman, "How is she today?"

The doctor hesitated before answering. "Fine, coming along."

"So you think it's healthy?"

"As far as I know, yes."

He nodded and left, but came back a few more times, asking similar questions. Olmstead and Saman figured he was biding his time, waiting to make a move. The exact nature of that move remained a mystery, which only made Olmstead more nervous.

The baby continued to grow, and the lieutenant spent much of her time thinking about all the different scenarios she might face once he arrived. She still worked as much as she could, but spent more time resting these days. Sometimes she read aloud or played music.

Funny, she thought, *I never saw myself as a mother before. No maternal instinct. And no one back home is allowed more than one child.* She smiled. *Well, at least I'll be acting within the law.*

As she thought more about this, Olmstead grew serious, then worried. *What will they do when they find out? I can't spend the rest of my life hiding out with my son. Will they take him away?*

One afternoon, Saman urged Olmstead to take the "wait and see" attitude, but this hardly satisfied her. She cradled her swelling abdomen with both hands, then began pacing.

Suddenly, she heard a commotion outside and rushed to

the force field. Parry had burst in with two security guards right behind him — but Olmstead realized they weren't with him; they were *after* him. His eyes were wild as he breathed hard, sweating and clutching a gun at his side.

"What's going on?" Saman demanded to know.

"Captain Parry wanted to put the ship on auto-destruct," the first guard said, "with no explanation. He tried to make the Second Officer give consent, but he refused. The captain lost control and attacked him, then ran from the Control Center."

"You don't know what's at stake here," Parry said, catching his breath. His eyes darted from one person to another. "I'm trying to save our families and friends back home —"

"By destroying this ship?" Saman countered. She glanced at Olmstead. The lieutenant retreated to the far end of the Q-Wing, crouching down behind her bed, but she still had a clear view of everything. The captain was right outside.

"Lieutenant Olmstead is endangering us," Parry insisted. "She's harboring an alien inside her body, and it will kill us all if we don't stop it."

The guards looked at each other in confusion. "Sir, we don't know what you're talking about," said the second one, "but if you'll calm down, we can discuss this."

"There's no time!" Parry shouted. In a quick motion, he disabled the force field using the wall control. Olmstead tried to duck for cover as he aimed at her. The gun went off when the others lunged at him, grabbing his arms; and the lieutenant screamed when the force beam grazed her.

The officers had drawn their own weapons, and they took him down with a narrow energy beam intended to wound him. He fell to the floor, writhing and crying out in pain. Saman snatched his weapon away.

One of the guards helped the doctor lift Parry onto an exam table, while the other guard rushed over to Olmstead. "Oh, God — are you okay?"

She winced. "I think so. I'm not sure."

The guard looked down, noticing her rounded belly, then glanced up at her with an expression of both puzzlement and worry.

"Make sure the captain is taken care of first," she told him.

"Then we'll fill you in."

⚗⚗

"Well, the report is making its rounds," Saman told Olmstead the next day. "Lying isn't something I'm proud of, but everyone's buying it — for now."

Olmstead and the baby had come through the attack with no serious harm. As far as everyone else on *The New Hope* was now concerned, she'd become pregnant by a man on board, and they'd decided not to reveal his identity. The scuttlebutt and denials swirled, but no one drew any conclusions.

Saman had also reported success in eradicating Olmstead's illness; she no longer needed to stay in the Q-Wing. Some of her crewmates regarded her with disdain, but most of them supported her. A few offered to throw a shower when they got back home.

"We'll see," she said aloud — then thought, *If you only knew.*

The doctor did her best to heal Parry's wounds, then quarantined him for a while, keeping him under constant guard. According to the record, he'd contracted a virus on Planet T-75 which had lain dormant, undetected until recently. Then it had begun affecting his mental processes, causing acute paranoia, delusions and hostility — all made worse by the pressures placed on him to find a new home for humanity.

After a few days, Saman expressed concern about the large doses of medications he required and ordered him put into suspension to save resources. They had only a short journey home now, no more than a week, and the Second Officer was more than qualified to handle things.

"When they wake him and he starts talking again, you and I can kiss our careers good-bye," Olmstead told Saman.

"That's a chance I'm prepared to take."

A few days later, just as they entered Earth's orbit, Olmstead went into labor. She called for help and made it into the medical chamber with two crewmembers at her side. Saman dismissed them and said she'd call for a nurse — then stopped and told Olmstead, "You and I'll have to do this on our own; the baby's coming faster than any I've ever delivered before. Looks like Alexander can't wait."

The lieutenant felt almost no pain except during the final

push — and then the large infant slipped into Saman's hands. She snipped the umbilical cord and smiled.

The baby's skin was cobalt blue, hairless, and its golden eyes glittered under the lights. No sound came from the thin mouth, but the baby turned its head and looked from the doctor to Olmstead, apparently able to focus on them already.

"Eight fingers, eight toes," Saman announced, touching the wide, flat hands and feet. The chest and nostrils moved, signaling that Alexander was breathing.

"Why isn't he crying?" Olmstead asked, worried.

"Maybe his species doesn't do that," Saman said. "He's awfully strong, though. Oh my God, he's —"

The baby had begun expanding in size — slowly at first, then so rapidly that Saman had to rush to the next table and put him down before she dropped him. Neither woman could speak as Alexander stretched himself out and grew to a height of five feet. Then he sat up and faced them.

"Thank you, Pamela — my second mother, and Doctor Saman," he said in a smooth, pleasant voice, speaking as well as anyone on board. He got off the table and approached Olmstead, taking her hands in his. "Congratulations."

"What — what are you talking about?" his mother said, barely able to get the words out. "How could you grow that fast and be able to speak already? Why — "

"Sshhh," he said gently, stroking her face. "I'm sorry I couldn't tell you anything earlier. You — both of you — deserve an explanation."

They listened as he continued. "My race lives on a planet near the one you intended to colonize. We listened to many of your transmissions, translated them, and learned that humans have severely damaged their own world. My people feared that you might do the same to a colony, then move on again — only to destroy another planet.

"Long ago, we were once as destructive as you are; and, although we're far from perfect, we wish to share our knowledge, experience, and technology with you to try to help humans salvage their home planet. We don't believe that you are ready yet for colonization."

"But if that was your intention all along," asked Saman, "why didn't you tell us sooner?"

"You had to prove that you deserved some consideration," Alexander told her. "You could have killed me yourself, but you didn't. I took that to be partly representative of your species. Then your captain tried to kill me; and, although he did not succeed, he also displayed a typical human behavior. My superiors had said that you have a great capacity for violence; but also that if you're still capable of mercy and of changing the way you think, there may be hope for you."

"How could you have put yourself at such risk?" asked Olmstead. "Were you forced to be part of this experiment?"

Alexander shook his head. "No one is ever forced to take such drastic measures. As an adult capable of making my own decisions, I volunteered to go through the reduction and rebirth process, to take the risks, because I believed in your people."

Olmstead felt ashamed. "At first, I didn't want you. I was afraid."

"I know, and I understood that. But I believed in you too, Pamela — and you didn't disappoint me."

"I'm concerned about the others," Saman said. "I don't know how they'll take it — on this ship or on Earth. Some people will think you're arrogant or dangerous."

"It won't be easy," Alexander replied. "I will send a message to my people to inform them of everything that has transpired. Soon they will arrive on Earth, but not everyone will be ready to receive them — just as your Captain Parry wasn't ready for me. We may have a very long and difficult path to follow."

"What about us?" Olmstead asked. "You and me. You're already an adult, with a lot of work ahead of you. I don't know where I'll fit in now."

"You'll be with me," he said. "We'll work together. I'll never leave you. How could I?"

Olmstead sighed with relief, then asked, "What's your real name?"

He chuckled. "It's quite long, and I'm not sure you could pronounce it. But I'll have plenty of time to teach it to you."

The three of them smiled; and somehow, as Olmstead gazed at her new son, she knew she wouldn't mind all the work ahead of her.

The Builder
Ellen Straw

"You heard me. Retreat *now.*"

Captain Jordan Acosta knew that his sharp tone and the look in his dark brown eyes would leave no doubt in anyone's mind. The landing party gathered up their materials and ran out of the blue-green forest towards their scarred, dark gray battleship, the *Crusader,* which hovered in a nearby clearing. They'd battled a Venkrian vessel the day before, but before they finally ran it off, they'd suffered several casualties and used up a good portion of their supplies and equipment. And now that they were on the ground trying to replenish their resources, Venkrian reinforcements were on the way, with Earth vessels right behind them.

The Earth Force ships were as far from their home planet as their enemies were from theirs, but none of them was ever far from Border Planet Three. The Venkrians wanted this particular planet badly and were intent on plundering its natural resources. It also lay in disputed territory. When the Venkrian Empire had declared it their property, that was more than enough to make the Earth Force Supreme Commanders order their battleship captains to take turns defending it between skirmishes.

And we've damn near lost it, Acosta thought bitterly, helping his people scramble back onto the ship.

His First Officer, Commander Gwen Mullins, came running towards him. She was breathing hard, wisps of her red hair sticking to her sweaty face. "Captain, we're missing Lieutenant Pierce, and he didn't respond to my call. I want to take a Security team and go back for him."

Acosta shook his head. "I'll go. Tell Medical to prepare for...."

He couldn't finish the sentence, couldn't say the words *another casualty*. He'd known Pierce for a long time. He also knew the man was well known for risking his own safety by working to the very last minute.

Mullins nodded. The captain called for two Security officers, and they ran for the edge of the forest.

They'd only been scanning for a few minutes when they found Pierce lying facedown in the grass behind a boulder, not moving, his light-skinned face and unruly blond hair wet with perspiration, a nasty lump already visible on his forehead.

"Prepare to leave as soon as we're on board," Acosta told Mullins by transceiver. They lifted the unconscious man and carried him back to the ship; and, after leaving Pierce in Medical, Acosta headed for Command.

The captain's expression remained somber as they traveled a safe distance away. Part of him wanted to stay in the battle zone, supporting the other units. But the *Crusader* couldn't take another pounding. Not for a while.

He looked around Command at the tired faces of his crew. They appeared as beaten-up as their ship did these days, and on the verge of losing their tempers if they so much as bumped into each other. He wouldn't blame them if they did. It was hard to move around the small, steel-gray Command area, whose design had been based on that of old Earth submarines; and they'd all been under considerable strain. Four people had died in the latest skirmish as well.

Mullins came up next to him. "I know you hate it when we crawl away and lick our wounds," she said quietly. "It's just our turn, sir. We don't have a choice."

Acosta sighed, staring straight ahead. "How many more turns do we have to take? This has been going on for months. They're relentless. I shouldn't say this, but sometimes I wish...."

"That Earth Forces would just give them the damn planet already," Mullins finished for him.

He turned and looked at her. "You always seem to know exactly what I'm thinking."

"What's a First Officer for?"

Acosta managed a smile. "For taking over Command. I'm going to pay a visit to Medical and then my quarters to clean up.

I'll be back later."

He felt her green eyes watching him as he left.

☊⅍

"So it's not serious?" Acosta asked, cocking his head towards Pierce. The lieutenant was sitting up in bed, clutching a cold pack to his head, his eyes closed.

"Nothing that some ice and anti-inflammatory meds won't take care of," replied Dr. Yolanda Clarence, a tall black woman with exotic features. "He doesn't remember how it happened."

"Isn't that strange?"

The doctor shrugged. "Not necessarily. There were a lot of rocks around. He might have tripped when he was running for the ship and hit his head on one. Or he might have blacked out for a second. He doesn't have a history of neurological problems, but they can appear all of a sudden. Nothing showed up on any of my scans, though." She gave Acosta an apologetic look. "I wish I had better answers for you, sir."

"Sometimes there aren't any answers, Yolanda. When can he go back on duty?"

"Tomorrow morning, if he's up for it. I want him to rest in his quarters today after I release him."

"Good enough. Thank you, Doctor."

The captain approached Pierce after Clarence went back into her office. "How are you feeling, Andy?"

Pierce jumped a little, as if he'd been caught doing something wrong. He opened his blue eyes and adjusted the pack. "Like a liability, Captain. I'll be all right. Didn't hit anything I use."

The captain had to smile at that. "You always were a hardhead."

"And this hardhead is going back on duty in eighteen hours, sir."

Acosta studied him for a minute. Pierce's eyes had an odd, faraway look in them, as if he were concentrating hard on something — or worrying. "What's wrong, Lieutenant?"

"Oh, nothing, sir. Sorry. I was just trying to figure out how I could have knocked myself unconscious. I didn't mean to make trouble for anyone — no more than usual, that is."

"Rescuing a crewmember is never trouble. Don't worry about

it. Just take it easy. I guess you heard we're not going anywhere for a while."

Pierce nodded. "We're regrouping again."

"It's getting to be a regular pattern," Acosta muttered. "Feel better, Andy. I'll see you later."

"Thank you, sir."

Acosta headed for the door, then turned around at the last minute to take one more look at Pierce. The man now wore a grim expression.

The painkillers just haven't kicked in yet, Acosta told himself, on his way to his quarters. *You know what that's like.* He'd taken them frequently during this war, for severe headaches, and would take them again when he had to sit down and write letters of condolence to the families of those among his crew who had died.

Acosta was glad to rid himself of his grimy clothes. He could only bear the sweat, dirt and grime for so long. *I wish there were a way to clean it off the ship*, he thought.

After stepping out of the shower, he wrapped a towel around his waist and walked over to his sink. A mirror hung over it, and he gazed at the reflection of smooth brown skin, thick black hair, and the muscles he tried to tone as often as possible.

"What good are muscles?" he said aloud, then thought of the Venkrians, which towered over humans and looked like a cross between a wild dog and a bear. "I can't fight those bastards with my bare hands. We need better weapons and more of them. Otherwise — "

He couldn't say the rest of it out loud. *They'll defeat us. The status reports don't look good, and everybody knows it. Assuming the Venkrians don't destroy all our ships, we'll be pushed back, into our own little patch of space, and they'll be free to plunder all the planets they can find and enslave the inhabitants — starting with us.*

Acosta shook his head and began drying himself. "Stop thinking about it," he spoke aloud again. "If you don't, Mullins will see the look on your face and she'll know."

A few minutes later, he grabbed a clean uniform — dark brown jacket and boots, tan pants, off-white undershirt — and ran a comb quickly through his hair. *I need sleep*, he thought, yawning, *but it'll have to wait till later.*

He kept his feelings to himself long enough to relieve Mullins and take over Command. A minor squabble broke out later between two officers who'd gotten in each other's way. Acosta didn't see any point in putting it on their records. He sent them away to cool off, then decided to change the entire duty shift. He was glad when it was over and he could finally get some rest.

⚏

The next morning, Acosta received a call from Dr. Clarence. "Captain, please meet me at Lieutenant Pierce's quarters," she said. "Something's wrong, and I can't explain it yet. You need to see it."

He acknowledged her immediately and left.

When he got there, the door was open and Clarence was standing just inside, her arms folded, her mouth set in a tight line. She barely looked up as the captain entered, and he stopped when he saw what Pierce was doing.

The lieutenant sat cross-legged on the floor, an array of tools, computer chips, metal panels, and other items spread out around him. Acosta knew he'd probably gotten it without much trouble, since he had Level One clearance and had specialized in both weaponry and computer systems.

What the captain couldn't understand was the significance of the object Pierce was building. It was comprised, so far, of a metal base and several computer chips — but he'd never seen anything like it and had no basis for comparison. Acosta knew something was terribly wrong. This wasn't normal behavior for Pierce, who had a clean record and no history of mental aberrances.

"How long has he been at this?" he asked Clarence.

"I'm not sure, Captain. He might have started yesterday or last night. When he didn't report for duty this morning or respond to any calls, his supervisor came here, took one look at him and called me. I've been watching him for about ten minutes. He won't answer questions, won't look up — just keeps on working."

She paused for a moment, then added, "I have a sedative injector with me, sir. Shall I use it?"

"No, not yet. But have it on hand, and call Security. Tell

159

them to come here and stand ready behind you."

As the doctor complied, Acosta moved slowly towards the officer until he was right next to him. Pierce's face was slick with sweat, and he looked weary but driven.

"Mister Pierce," Acosta said firmly, "I want you to stand up and face me."

The man continued working intently, quietly, stopping only to rub his eyes or wipe perspiration from his brow, wincing when he rubbed the purplish bruise.

Acosta raised his voice to see if he could get the lieutenant's attention. "Did you hear me, Pierce? Stop what you're doing right now. You'll only get yourself into more trouble if you don't."

He wasn't surprised when Pierce ignored him. Acosta glanced at Clarence, who stepped closer, ready to inject Pierce if necessary. Two Security guards had joined her.

The captain crouched down next to the lieutenant. "Andy," he said in a softer tone, "please tell me what's going on. We're worried about you. We just want to help."

Pierce stopped for a moment and gave Acosta a confused look. "I can't, sir," he said, in a voice just above a whisper — then returned to his task.

Acosta wasn't willing to give up yet. He put a hand on Pierce's shoulder. "You don't look good. At least take a break for a while."

Pierce shook his head. "Don't have time."

"Then tell me what you're building."

No response.

"Why are you doing it?"

"I have to."

"Are you under orders?"

"No, sir."

"I need an answer from you, Andy."

No reply.

The captain reached for the object, but Pierce grabbed his wrist firmly and forced him away from it.

Acosta stood up. "I don't know what's gotten into you, but for your sake this has to stop." He nodded to Clarence, who approached Pierce from the other side and pressed the pressure injector into his neck.

It had no effect at all.

The doctor regarded him with stunned disbelief, then looked up at the captain. "Sir, I put enough in there to knock him out for the rest of the day. And there's nothing wrong with our drug supply."

"I believe you, Doctor," Acosta murmured, "but we're dealing with something new here."

He motioned her aside and nodded to the guards, who came forward and grabbed hold of Pierce's arms to pull him to his feet. The lieutenant cried out, and in an incredible burst of strength, he broke free and threw one of them against the wall, then slammed the second one to the floor.

"Grab one gun. I'll get the other," Acosta told Clarence. "Level Three Stun at my signal." She looked reluctant, but obeyed.

When they were standing with guns pointed at Pierce, who sat between them, again at work on his project, Acosta spoke once more. "Lieutenant, we don't want to hurt you, but we will if you force the issue. Go with Dr. Clarence right now and we won't fire."

Pierce didn't look up. "I'm sorry, Captain."

Acosta's face fell. "I'm sorry too, Andy."

He nodded to Clarence, and they fired simultaneously. It had no more effect than the injection had.

"Oh my God," the doctor said under her breath, as the gun fell from her hand. She looked at Acosta. "What are we going to do with him now, sir?"

He couldn't answer her.

"Forget it, Gwen; you can't reason with him. And you don't have to whisper; he's tuned us out."

Ten minutes after the dual stun beams had been fired into his body at the highest possible force, Andy Pierce showed no sign of slowing down. He was shaky and pale from not having eaten or drunk much in hours, but appeared to be concentrating on some detailed work involving tiny circuits, relays and connections. The object now resembled a multi-pointed star, with additional points emerging from the center. Occasionally he gripped it with both hands for a few seconds, closing his eyes, then let go.

Clarence had called for assistance getting the two unconscious guards to Medical, then decided she might as well go back with them, as she had no reason to linger in Pierce's quarters. In the meantime, Acosta had summoned Mullins from Command and filled her in on what had just transpired. He stood with his arms folded, frowning as he tried to come up with a solution.

"Captain, was Pierce alone on that planet for any length of time?" asked Mullins.

"I don't know. Some worked in pairs, some worked alone. Andy was probably on his own, scanning for natural power sources. Why?"

"You and Dr. Clarence have theories, but you don't have any evidence of what actually went on down there," the commander stated.

Acosta looked at her. Somehow he felt it necessary to defend himself. "I don't know what you think could have happened, but there was no one on BP-3 except us. No life forms except the native flora and fauna, and the Venkrians hadn't arrived yet."

"Sir, I'm not saying anyone there influenced him —"

"Then what *are* you saying?" Acosta snapped.

"I'm telling you to look at what's right in front of you." She pointed at Pierce, whose hands now trembled as he held onto the object again, then let go. "He's obviously working on something that's beyond our understanding and could be very dangerous and powerful. He knows his way around weapons and computers better than anyone on board except you and me. If what he's building is supposed to benefit us, why hasn't he let us in on it?"

Acosta's voice rose in anger. "Jesus! What do you think he is, some kind of spy? He's human, in case you hadn't noticed."

"Then how do you account for his being able to withstand sedatives and stun guns?"

"Genetic modifications, I suppose. Earth Forces has covert scientific operations and laboratories — you know that. I couldn't begin to guess what goes on in them."

"You're guessing right *now*, Captain. Making assumptions. How do you even know he's on our side? He could have sold out; it's been known to happen."

"Christ, Mullins. I suppose you think he knocked himself

unconscious too. What's gotten into you?"

"I'm doing exactly what I'm supposed to do: playing devil's advocate."

"It doesn't sound like that to me, Commander. You're making accusations."

"It's suspicious activity, sir."

"All right, that's enough." The captain glared at her as he continued. "I've known Andy for years, and he's no spy. At first I thought Clarence had missed something in her scans, or that Pierce's head injury caused behavioral changes later that she never expected. The more likely possibility is that he's working undercover for Earth Forces and was told not to reveal his objectives to us until a certain time."

"Then what do you think he's working on?"

"Some kind of communications device."

"You're a battleship captain, a strategist. Why wouldn't they have told you about it?"

"The fewer people who know about something like this, the better." Acosta shot Mullins a look daring her to press the issue.

She met his gaze head-on. "Is that another one of your theories, sir? Are you planning to just let him run things from now on?"

He shook his head, trying to maintain his temper. "You've just crossed the line, Mullins. This is going on record."

She regarded him with disbelief. "You're writing me up for this?"

"Yes. And you'd better get out of here and back to Command before I change my mind and lock you away for the next few weeks."

The captain saw her jaw clench as she struggled not to flare up at him. Then she hurried out of the room.

Acosta leaned against the wall and rubbed his eyes, all his feelings now flooding his body at once: fatigue, anger, regret, frustration, doubt. He'd never felt more alone than at this moment.

The anger rose up inside him, and he strode over to where Pierce was working. "I hope you're satisfied, Lieutenant," he said harshly. "You've always had an obsessive streak. You've kept me in the dark, Mullins thinks you're against us, and I can't waste any more time watching you put together your damn contraption."

On impulse, Acosta kicked the star-like object with all his might and sent it flying. Then he stepped back, bracing himself for potential retaliation.

The lieutenant made no hostile moves. He simply retrieved the apparatus, which hadn't been damaged, and put it back in its place, holding it for a few seconds.

The captain shook his head. "You don't hear what we say, you don't care what we do, you don't give a damn if this war kills all of us. The hell with you." He started for the door.

Pierce's words stopped him: "I care, Captain. I'm not your enemy, and I'm not working undercover."

Acosta couldn't believe the lieutenant was actually facing him. Pierce had dark patches under the eyes, and his voice was raspy. The captain approached him, kneeling next to him so they were at the same eye-level when Pierce turned to face him. "Andy, what happened to you on Border Planet Three?"

"Prael."

"What?"

Pierce took a deep breath. "That's the planet's name, sir. There's a race of people living on it. The Praelites are tiny, with no limbs, but highly intelligent. When I was searching for energy resources and no one else was around, they contacted me telepathically and we communicated. Then they transferred some of their knowledge into my mind and their powers into my body. I consented to it. The process was so overwhelming and so rapid that I lost consciousness and hit my head when I fell. They needed someone to be their arms and eyes, to build this device —"

"Wait a minute," the captain interrupted. "What *is* this device? If they needed our help, why didn't they contact the rest of us? Did they force you to do this?"

Pierce hesitated before responding, apparently trying to muster up the energy to continue. When he began to slump over, Acosta held him up until he recovered. "It's a ship disabler, sir. It can be used against an entire fleet of ships all at once, even if they're nowhere near us. We can bring the Venkrians to their knees."

"How do you know the Praelites don't intend to harm *us* with it?"

"We made a deal, Captain. They gave me this weapon in exchange for my keeping their existence secret for a while. They're aware of our war, and they know the Venkrians want Prael for its resources. If they find out about the Praelites' existence, they'll either enslave or destroy them all. You know that. When we were communicating, the Praelites learned a few things about humans: that we want to defeat the enemy and preserve as many lives as we can, and that we wouldn't try to conquer their world."

Pierce stopped again for a moment, then resumed. "I agreed to this, sir. I *want* to do it, to prove myself to the Praelites and end this war."

"But it's killing you. I can see it in your face. Anyone could."

"I know I might die. I already agreed to the risk. Every time I put my hands on this thing, it takes more life energy out of me. But I don't have anyone to leave behind, sir. The Venkrians saw to that when they wiped out my family. You know that."

"Andy —"

"You can't talk me out of it," Pierce said. "You know how stubborn I am."

Acosta shook his head, perplexed. "You're going to risk your life for a race of people you just met?"

"Not only for them. For thousands of humans. And Venkrians, for that matter, when the fighting stops. Measure my life against all the lives that will be saved. It's worth it. You and I are soldiers, sir. We signed up for this. We knew there might come a time when we'd have to sacrifice ourselves. Well, this is it. This is my time."

Seeing the hope and determination in Pierce's eyes, Acosta knew he couldn't be swayed. The captain remained silent for a moment, then said quietly, "I think you just want to get your name in the history books."

Pierce smiled. "That's it, exactly." He made another adjustment to the object, then asked, "Don't you trust Mullins anymore?"

"I don't know. You heard what she said."

"She was doing her job, sir. Sometimes she just does it a

little too well. I think you can still trust her."

Acosta considered this. "Maybe so."

The lieutenant placed his hands on the disabler once more, then said, "It's ready, Captain. I need to get it to Weapons Control."

Acosta nodded, then pulled Pierce to his feet as the latter held on to the object. The lieutenant limped, leaning against his commanding officer for support as they headed down the corridor, ignoring the stares and whispers they drew from others.

When they arrived at Weapons, Acosta dismissed everyone on duty and helped Pierce to a chair. Next, the captain sealed the door shut and implemented his private codes to thwart any attempts to stop him. He applied manual controls to send the ship back into the heart of the battle zone as quickly as possible. Then he turned to Pierce with a questioning look.

"Help me over to the main console, sir."

In a matter of minutes, the lieutenant performed a series of complex tasks that his captain couldn't begin to comprehend. The device now produced an eerie yellow glow and emitted a low hum.

"What can I do?" asked Acosta.

"Just tell me when we're there, Captain. Don't put the shields up — and don't let me fall."

A short time later, they reached an area of space notorious for its heavy Venkrian patrols. "It's time, Andy," the captain said. "They'll be coming at us any minute now."

No sooner had Pierce spoken than three Venkrian ships appeared on the sensors. The lieutenant took a deep breath, gripped the disabler as tightly as he could, and squeezed his eyes shut. A series of yellow energy streams surged from the *Crusader*, some striking the attacking vessels while others continued into open space.

Acosta was so astonished that he could barely force himself to look away long enough to call his First Officer on the main comm unit. "Acosta to Mullins. Can you see what's going on out there?"

"I see it, Captain," she replied slowly, sounding as if she were trying to recover from shock. "I just can't believe it. Whatever you and Pierce have done, it's working. Our sensors indicate that the Venkrian ships have lost all their power. Wait, there's a message coming in...."

The line was silent for a few moments, and then Acosta smiled when he heard cheers and clapping coming from Command. "Sir, we're getting reports from our other units. They say that all the Venkrian commanders are calling and begging for mercy. They're powerless. We've beaten them!"

"With a little help from the Praelites," Acosta told her, smiling.

"Sir?"

"I'll explain later."

His smile faded when Pierce slumped and he had to lower the officer to the floor. "Andy, did you hear that? The war is over. You did it."

Pierce's eyes had glazed over, but a faint smile appeared on his face. "*We* did it," he whispered, barely audible. "Sir... please go back to Prael.... Help me keep my promise."

"I will, Andy. I swear it."

Pierce took his last breath. His eyes closed, and he sagged in Acosta's arms.

⚐⚐

Later, Acosta and Mullins stood side by side in Medical as Dr. Clarence finished readying Pierce's body for transport back to Earth for a proper burial. The *Crusader* was on its way to Prael.

"Another death, another letter of condolence to write," the captain said. "But at least his family will know that Andy's sacrifice ended a war."

Mullins looked shame-faced. "Sir... I shouldn't have suggested that he was a traitor."

"And I shouldn't have dismissed your concerns," Acosta replied gently, leading her towards the door. "I learned from Andy not to assume you know the whole story when you don't have all the facts." He paused, then added, "By the way, Gwen... I never wrote you up."

The First Officer smiled. "Well, then, it'll be easier for me to find a new job in peacetime."

He returned the smile, and they walked out together.

Ellen Straw

These stories grew out of my imagining of relationships and challenges faced by those who live on spaceships. I have used this particular setting for many stories. Along with being a writer, I am a college English professor, editor and proofreader, agitator and organizer, movie buff, Internet junkie, casino maven, and sitter for houses, dogs, kids, and the elderly.

A Jolt to the System
Margaret Yang and Harry R. Campion

Arnold Reale's first jolt of the day hit him at the bottom of his apartment stairs. The source was a decrepit bum — homeless person, he corrected himself with a tired shake of his head — camped out on the stoop and staring at Arnold's suit and shoes as if in amazement.

— *had shoes like that, when I worked at Penney's.* It was cold. He was lying on his side on the freezing pavement, staring at the corner of the dumpster. He could see the rust pattern on the dumpster very clearly. It looked like a face, looking back at him with empty eyes. There was an icicle connecting the dumpster to the ground like a tiny crystal support pillar. It was so cold. He tried to pull his coat closer around him, but his fingers wouldn't hold the fabric. They were numb, and growing distant. Everything was growing distant.

Arnold shook himself all over as if he could still feel the man freezing. He deliberately looked up into the clear autumn sky over Manhattan. Winter was still weeks away, and it wouldn't happen this winter anyway. Next? Next. He dropped a five-dollar bill in the man's cup and turned away.

The sidewalk became more crowded at the corner, like a stream trickling down to join a river. He swallowed, convinced that this was going to be one of *those* days, and plunged into the current.

Arnold's appearance was so vague that his mother once joked that he had trouble recognizing his own reflection. He didn't just blend into a crowd, he vanished without a trace. His clothing choices did not help: brown trench coat over equally uninspired brown suit and shoes, just another bit of flotsam swept away on the tide.

After three blocks, Arnold came to a sudden halt. The crowd flowed around him in a wave. Usually the press of so many strangers bothered Arnold in a way that made his skin itch, but now he simply stood still, staring at a man a block further down. The man stood on a milk crate, dressed in threadbare army fatigues and gesturing broadly to the indifferent crowd.

Not him again.

Arnold turned and pushed back up the street to the crosswalk, his briefcase suddenly a lead weight in his hand. He crossed to the other side of 116th Street and turned west again. His eyes darted back over the roofs of the cars, measuring and remeasuring the distance between himself and the man in the faded greens.

Far enough, Arnold thought. Maybe far enough. Don't look at him, don't think about him. You're almost past him... Against his will his eyes returned to the crate-elevated individual who was now directly across the street. A sigh of relief had just escaped him when the jolt came.

— and there SHALL be a day of reckoning before the LORD — send these stinking souls straight down to hell to burn and burn and burn the way they deserve and should and — He was hunched over the little table in the basement. The little table that had stood in the corner of his bedroom and held the picture of Jesus and the twelve disciples when he was little and the table that he had to sit at when he was bad and the table that he had to lie on sometimes. His fingers were stroking the modeling clay that was not modeling clay but could be because the detonators weren't in it yet and as long as the detonators weren't in it C4 was just like modeling clay or Play-Doh, or bread dough — Jesus took the bread and broke it saying this is my body and eat it and eat it and eat it —

The jolt was physical this time — there was no way to guard against the bad ones — and Arnold jerked like a trout on a flyline. His stomach cramped and threatened to spill his breakfast out into the gutter. His briefcase fell from his nerveless fingers and his hands clutched at his shoulders. Forget dignity. Time to run. He snatched up his briefcase and sprinted down the sidewalk, not feeling the elbows and shoulders, not hearing the muttered curses and oaths directed at him. The panic receded with distance.

He turned into the subway entrance and caught his breath on the top stair. He was five steps down before he changed his mind. No, on one of *those* days the subway would be unendurable. He'd probably jolt on every person riding his train and all the oncoming ones too. Arnold swam up to the surface and hailed a taxi. He should have just enough money to get to work.

"Forty-eighth and Lexington," he said as he climbed through the door. He settled into the seat as the driver took off, swiveling into traffic like a pinball.

Arnold caught a glimpse of his own face in the rear view mirror: drawn and pale. He leaned forward, resting his elbows on his knees and cradling his face in his hands. He wiped the sheen of sweat from his upper lip with the back of his hand.

— *another friggin' drunk. He pukes in my cab and I'll wipe it up with his* —

"Just drive," Arnold muttered. He pressed his hands tight against his head as if to form a barrier. He pictured a strong box locking away his emotions. He stared into the blankness of his palms, concentrating on them. He wouldn't go where this man was taking him. Relax. Relax. It took all his concentration to keep the jolt away, to keep everything in its little box.

By the time he got to work, he was calm again, the khaki man and his milk crate almost forgotten. The elevator up to the 40th floor was the usual series of mundane jolts. "I bought a lottery ticket," one woman told her friend. "It's up to 13 million." You won't win, Arnold thought.

"I'm going to Florida next week," another said. You'll have a wonderful time, Arnold thought. "I'll show you the pictures when I get back." Seen them.

"Jill and I are going out tonight," one executive confided to another with a smirk. Arnold stared hard at him. You're going to spill wine on her at dinner and get slapped on the doorstep. Cretin.

Sometimes Arnold felt the compulsion to tell them what he knew, what he saw. Go ahead, the nasty little voice within him whispered, tell them all about it. They probably think they want to know, so tell them. Tell them *all* about it.

Not today.

The elevator opened onto the corporate logo of Plante and

Moran. He shuffled through the door with the morning crowd.

"Good morning, Arnold," ventured Beth Butterfield, peeking out of the mouse-hole of her cubicle. When she smiled, which was seldom enough, her wan face dimpled and became something lovely. "How was your weekend?" she asked.

"Short," he said regretfully. "Yours?"

"Oh, same old, same old." Movie marathon on American Movie Classics. Take-out pizza. Comfortable sweats and her cat. He loved the mild impressions from Beth, could almost curl up in their comforting blandness. Her life was simple, relaxed, content. "Best get some work done," she said with a wave.

Arnold smelled the coffee Beth started every morning and wished for a cup. But today, elbowing for position at the cream and sugar held little attraction. He stared at the floor until he was safely in his cubicle.

Arnold's first appointment of the day was early. Meeting clients had to be the worst part of accounting. He was usually content to hide in his tiny cubicle and work on numbers. Numbers never jolted him. Sometimes, however, he had to see clients.

Ted Watkowski, head of the fledgling SuperFar golf ball company, had kept his books at Plante and Moran for five years. Watkowski had stopped trying to shake hands with Arnold and never sat too close. "Here are September's final figures," Watkowski said. "Let's see how we close out the quarter." Arnold took out the SuperFar company's file and opened to the third quarter statement.

At that moment, a head prairie-dogged above the cubicle divider in front of him. Ralph. "Hi Arnie," Ralph said. "Busy?"

Arnold looked pointedly at Mr. Watkowski, contenting himself with thoughts of Ralph's forthcoming vasectomy. "Yes."

"Have you picked up your mail yet?"

"No." Not until after ten, when the rush was over. "I'll look at it later."

"Okay," Ralph said. "Let me know when." The head withdrew.

"Sorry about that," Arnold said to Watkowski. "Now, let me have a look at that statement."

Arnold was entering the SuperFar data into the computer when the jolt came. — *poor little guy probably hasn't been laid since high school. He should work out* — He was lying on his back and watching the stars and the dark sky vanish into morning. He could feel nothing, not the ground beneath him, nor his twisted and crumpled body, not even the dew condensing on his still-open eyes. His last thoughts were of the fifty thousand dollars, a stack of bills as high as the bridge that rose and towered above him, the bridge that was fading into a new darkness that fell over the morning sky, engulfing the stars and the bridge and the world, and, of course, him.

Arnold turned to Watkowski in surprise, then back to his computer. There it was, the missing fifty thousand dollars. Watkowski hadn't even tried to conceal it. Now what? "Mr. Watkowski," he said slowly, evenly. "There's an error in your calculations. If I can see this fifty thousand dollar withdrawal, anyone can."

"So?"

"So, you've got to report it as personal income."

"But I'm head of the company," Watkowski said defensively. "It's my money."

"That's really not a problem, Mr. Watkowski. Call it a bonus, call it a disbursement, but report it to the IRS."

Watkowski sat back in his chair, shaking his head. "But if I take it this way, I won't have to fork over a third of it in taxes."

"Mr. Watkowski, embezzlement is one thing, tax evasion is another. I'd hate to see you go to jail over this." Or off a bridge, he thought. Arnold walked around in another jolt for a few seconds. Was the bridge gone? It was hard to say… maybe. "Take whatever you think you need," Arnold said. "But report it."

"Arnie?" The talking head was back. "Big news, Arnie."

"Not now, Ralph."

Arnold stared at Ted Watkowski, waiting. Watkowski stared back for a moment, then threw up his hands in defeat. "Whatever. Do whatever, Reale." He shook his head, mumbling something about the damned government's thousand dollar toasters.

Arnold worked out a bonus plan for the SuperFar company that would minimize his client's tax liability, and sent Watkowski on his way within twenty minutes. He tossed the paperwork into his "out" basket, took a deep breath, and walked next door to Ralph's cubicle.

Ralph was just draining the contents of his Eiffel tower (genuine souvenir of Paris) coffee mug. Arnold looked wistfully at the coffee. Maybe later. "Okay, Ralph, what is it?"

"You haven't been to your mail box yet today?"

"Not yet." I've been busy doing my job, you silly twit.

"Well, uh. The transfers came out today —"

Arnold felt a smile tug at the corners of his mouth. Finally, he thought. Finally some good news. After nine years in this hell-hole, after five years of requests. Finally. He forced himself to calm, knowing the consequences of letting his enthusiasm get away from him.

"Apparently I've been downsized," Ralph said. "Can you believe it? They're sending me out to Ellinwood. Ellin-stinking-Wood, can you believe?"

Arnold felt his tight, controlled box of thoughts crack open a little in surprise, questing. He could never get a jolt about himself. Never. Even when he really, really needed one.

"What do you mean?" he heard himself ask. "You're being transferred?"

"Yeah," Ralph snorted in disgust. "Out to the butt-end of nowhere too. After all the time I put into my job, after all —"

"Ellinwood. But. But, I." Arnold looked around the office for a moment, disoriented. "But, *I'm* supposed to go to Ellinwood. That's the posting *I* requested." It wasn't fair. He'd done all he could. He'd stayed here as long as he could stand it, here in the city with the noise and the confusion and the *lives*, his one hope the escape to the suburbs.

"Oh no," Arnold mumbled. The box where he stored his emotions was leaking out the sides. He shook his head, feeling like a man denying a bad dream. "No no no. NO!" Ralph jumped as if stung. "You! You are not going anywhere! You are staying right here and doing your job in the same crappy way year after crappy year. I can see your retirement party, crappy gold watch and all!"

Faces peered curiously over and around the dividers. Arnold caught a low babble of intrigue from a dozen minds. He had futile thoughts of calm. Don't let it get to you, Arnold. Don't let it — but the prospect of another year, another two years, another *ten* in the city rose before him like a spectre.

"Hey pal, they stuck me with this transfer," Ralph protested. "Who in their right mind would want to go to Ellinwood?"

"In their right mind, Ralph?" Arnold demanded. "What the hell do you know about right minds? I'll tell you about people's minds!"

A few of his co-workers entered Ralph's cubicle and moved hesitantly toward Arnold, expressions filled with concern. "Get away from me!" he cried, but it wouldn't do any good. The box had broken open. He whirled on a co-worker. "Grace, going to Vegas? So much for the kids' college fund. Paul? Enjoy those smoking breaks while you can, pal. Eighteen months until they diagnose you. Radiation is *not* your friend. Peter, congrats on the game show. We're all going to be so proud of you, but get real! It's *Wheel of Fortune*, not *Jeopardy*. Anyone can get Marilyn Monroe with just the *vowels* missing!"

The jolts were coming fast and furious now, like a landslide in his head, an avalanche broken free and gaining speed on the downslope. He raced across the office to where a dark, good-looking fellow was talking on the phone. He snatched a framed portrait off the desktop and waved it in the man's face. "Your wife, Kent. *This* is your wife. Not the little hooker that you see every Tuesday. Venereal disease is *not* something to bring home like milk!"

Arnold spun out of Kent's cubicle and dashed into another one. "Gladys." he took the woman's hands. "You're a very nice person. I like you very much. But you're going to get mugged outside your apartment next week, beaten, and left for dead." He dropped her hands and wiped at the sweat pouring from his brow. "Can you see why I hate this?"

The jolts were coming in from the surrounding offices now, breaking over him in a wave, spiraling out and out to include the entire floor, the surrounding floors, the offices in the next building: a slideshow of joy and sorrow.

Arnold ran to the double-paned windows and hammered with his fist, trying ineffectually to attract the attention of the workers in the neighboring building.

"Hey Morty!" he cried. "How about doubling up on that fire insurance? Electrical fire in the attic around Christmas! Down in flames, buddy!"

Fear of the ever-expanding spiral stopped him at last. What if it just kept going out and going out until it reached 116th Street to jolt across the khaki-man again?

Or someone worse.

The return of his emotions to their little box inside him closed off the jolts as if shutting a door. A large and heavy door. Arnold rested his head against the cool glass of the window for a moment, staring down at the tiny streets below and their myriad of minuscule people, sweeping along toward who knew what.

He slowly turned to see a wall of faces staring at him. The office was silent but for the ringing of unheeded phones and an embarrassed shuffling of feet. Feeling a hot flush mount through his collar and up his cheeks, Arnold walked stiffly back to his cubicle.

He sat at his desk, staring at the dividers, ignoring the whispers from over the walls. Footsteps tiptoed past his door and then scurried around the corner. He stood and stared over the dividers. People suddenly looked down at their work or picked up the phone.

With a heavy sigh, Arnold marched into his boss' office and closed the door.

"Mr. Dillender, I have to leave." His voice was soft and steady.

Dillender drummed his fingertips on the desk. "Yes, of course, Reale. Take the rest of the day off."

"You don't understand. I have to get out of here. I need that transfer. My neighbor's husband is going to die in a few months. Do you think I need that kind of grief seeping through the walls?"

Dillender had apparently chosen not to listen. "I'm afraid the decision is already out of my hands," he said. "You're far too valuable to our —"

"I can't stay," Arnold said, his words were as measured and even as he could make them. "I either get the transfer or I'm taking that offer from Decker Mutual." He left his boss' office without waiting for a reply.

With an empty box from the copy room, Arnold sorted through his desk for his few personal items: address book, a paperweight, stamps, some mints.

Urgent whispers outside the divider. "...did he know I tried out for *Wheel of Fortune?*" and "…Kent's calling his wife right now." A woman from Personnel stood at the mouth of the cubicle.

"Mr. Reale?" She was wringing her hands together.

"Yes, Frances," he said quietly.

"I'm very sorry to bother you, but my husband and I are trying to have children and I was wondering —"

"Yes, Frances," he repeated.

"We — we will?" her eyes shone.

Stan walked in right behind Frances. "Arnold? You know that screenplay I've been working on?"

"You'll sell it, Stan. Keep writing. Bye."

He looked up. Ralph's face was once again peeking at him over the divider. "Arnie? I've been thinking a lot about how I'm afraid to fly? Am I going to die in a plane crash?"

"No! You're going to live in a retirement home for six years, working on your tan and lusting after the aerobics instructor." He made a face at Ralph. "You don't look good in leotards *now*. In 20 years? Yech!"

Arnold shoved aside the cardboard box and sat at his desk, head in hands, concentrating on breathing. In. Out. A steaming mug of coffee was set on the desk in front of him. He looked up. He'd been concentrating so hard on blocking out the world that he hadn't even heard Beth come in.

"Are you all right?" she asked.

"I guess so." He picked up the mug. "Thanks. I needed this."

"I know." She made no move to leave.

"Is there something else? Something you want to ask me? Something you want to know?"

Beth shrugged. "No."

And there wasn't, he knew. "You're the only thing about this place I'll miss, Beth," Arnold said, then flushed. He gestured at the half-filled box on his desk. "I can't wait to get out of here."

"I know how you feel."

Yeah, right.

⟠⟠

The streets were clean in Ellinwood. There were no overflowing dumpsters in the alleys because there were no alleys.

There was no shriek of harsh machinery or odor of stale urine drifting out of the subway because there was no subway. Every avenue was lined with budding trees. Every boulevard's median was crowded with spring flowers. The lawns were lovingly maintained. Cars were washed with a regularity that bordered on religion. Children were cherished, maintained and washed with slightly less attention but no less fervor.

The blue sky with its streamers of white cloud were unmarred by high-rises; the tallest building in Ellinwood was the three-story town hall. From the front windows of the Plante and Moran branch office the sign for the town offices was highly visible: *Welcome! to Ellinwood! A Community with Character.* The citizens of Ellinwood were an affable, civic-minded, cheerful lot who clasped new arrivals with their good right hands and dragged them home for dinner. They were a people at ease with each other and their surroundings. They blended so seamlessly with Ellinwood that it was hard to picture the town without them or them without their town.

Arnold hated it.

He had waited the entire winter, watching everyone trudge by in snow-boots and knit hats, waiting to be charmed by small town America.

He sat in his swivel chair in the 3-desk office, his elbows on his desk blotter. Shari, the perky receptionist, walked by his door. "You're not working late again, are you, Mr. Reale?"

Arnold looked at his watch. Yep, five o'clock. He could set the thing by her. He feigned surprise. "Is it that time already?"

Shari, ten years away from four squalling children, forty extra pounds and a quietly dying marriage, never failed to giggle at this. "That time. See you tomorrow." She was gone. The office was quiet but for the hum of the desktop computers. Arnold sighed.

He packed his briefcase with papers he didn't really need to review and locked the front door behind him. There was no alarm system.

Home was a two-mile walk from the office and Arnold never hurried. He thought about the evening's prospects. He'd eaten at home every day this week. A bite at the diner on Main Street? Maybe there'd be somebody new in town.

A string of bells jangled as he opened the door to the Main Street Diner. He took a seat at the counter between Bill Brady (who would lose next spring's school-board election) and Judge Hadley, (who'd moved to the suburbs on his doctor's advice and whose blood pressure had gone down to 160 over 70).

He greeted the men and placed his order with the waitress. She was thinking about her aching legs, he noted, yet again. They were getting worse, but the varicose veins weren't showing yet. She'd be shocked by the price of surgery, but too vain to resist.

As he ate the Wednesday special, a decidedly un-special meatloaf, he idly cast about for any unusual jolts, any *new* jolts. Come on, Arnold thought, surprise me. Elsie, you have a blind date tonight? Oh, he's a perfect gentleman, you'll like him. Shoot. And Phillip, going to go home and drink beer in the Barcalounger in front of the Yankee's game. Again. And sixteen-year-old Nancy, drinking Coke after Coke at the diner in hopes of running into the handsome biology teacher, who won't come in. Even the passersby out on the sidewalk were going home to staid spouses or generic dogs or kids who got B's and played little-league (second base).

He was greeted and returned greetings on his walk home. He passed by the Dunkin' Donuts where the town's only deputy was carefully guarding a stool and three creme-filled. He was having the same old daydreams of gunning down marauding desperadoes who frankly wouldn't be caught dead in a suburb like Ellinwood.

Arnold's house was a tiny brick ranch with a front lawn the size of a double bed. Next door, Bill stood frowning at Arnold's weed-infested plot. Bill was on a first-name basis with every blade of grass in his own yard, mowed every other day and high-fived the Chemlawn man after his weekly treatments. "Hello, neighbor," Bill said.

"Evening, Bill." Arnold ignored the accusing eye.

—hole. *Dragging down every property value on the street with that* — Christmas time and the kids were home from college. Eggnog, with rum, by the fireplace. Sweater for Sally. Football for Bill Junior. Jokes about shoveling the walk in front of the house turning into the same old argument —

Arnold pulled away from the jolt with distaste. How many times would he have to watch this?

The house was cold and dark. The answering machine sat like a brick beside the phone, the message light unwinking. Arnold moved from room to room, turning on lights as he went. He made himself a cup of herb tea and settled before the television. He surfed through channel after channel, rerun after rerun. Jolts from the surrounding houses reached him at odd intervals, but faintly, like distant channels he could barely receive.

After two hours of bad TV he drew himself a hot bath and pulled a novel off the shelf. It was the third time he'd tried to read it. It didn't interest him this time either.

He drained the tub and pulled on old jeans and a faded sweatshirt. He turned off the lights in his house one by one and went out by the screen porch. A trail began at the back of his yard, crossing several fields of public land. Arnold trudged the mile or so with his hands stuffed into the pockets of his sweatshirt. In the distance he could hear a rushing thrum; the highway that passed by the town.

Beneath a railroad viaduct, Arnold climbed the embankment of the overpass. He curled up in the waist-high grasses near the guardrail, hoping to catch a jolt of *something* interesting from a passing car. — *large gut on that man* — *forgot to walk the dog again* — *can't get this math homework* — *did I miss the exit?* — *should have left him ages ago* — They were always so fast, so fleeting, just a taste, never enough to fill.

After a while, Arnold slept.

⇗⇘

Arnold's new apartment was one of four in a thick-walled brownstone near Washington Square Park in the Village. The August sky above New York was a clear hard blue filled with buildings. Arnold relaxed his shoulders and let a series of minor jolts flow through him from the surrounding throng.

Despair. Misery. Joy. Anticipation. He glanced back up at his home, nodded and continued on his way.

Arnold stepped out to join the pedestrian flood on Bleecker Street. He was a drop of water in the river. He did not shy away from the stream of thought-picture-emotion or fight it off. It passed through him and over him and he went on.

A faint tinge of alarm touched him. Directly ahead on the sidewalk was a terribly earnest young man with his hair pulled back in a dirty ponytail and John Lennon glasses.

"We're dying in our own waste heat! The mean temperature has risen ten degrees in the last five years. At this rate the polar ice caps will melt in another twenty years! This whole city will be under water — warm water!" The young man was waving a handful of pamphlets at everyone walking by. No one was taking them.

Arnold could feel the undercurrent of the man's fanatical jolt hovering on the edge of his mind. He spun around smoothly and skirted up La Guardia Place, keeping a large apartment complex between them. The blare of traffic and the tight confines of the sidewalk were now insular: not distracting, merely sustaining.

A neatly groomed man in a white Oxford shirt buttoned to the neck — no tie — grazed Arnold's shoulder in passing.

— *is he looking? Is he looking at me? Does he know? Does he? No of course not. No one knows. Fool them all. Fool them all.* He was standing and watching the girl's window, waiting for her silhouette to pass across that orange rectangle of light. Waiting for her to appear in the doorway. Waiting for her to take off her clothes. Waiting for the right moment. Waiting.

Arnold turned to see the man disappear around the corner and the jolt faded away. He shrugged and nearly smiled. One crazed peeping Tom can make your whole day.

One of *those* days again. Hmm. Arnold paused at the top of the subway entrance, dithering. There were a lot of people on the subway, perhaps more than he could handle on a day like today. Did he have enough money for a taxi?

"Mr. Reale."

He turned. Beth Butterfield stood behind him in a light summery suit. Its warm peach color lent her face the freshness of a sun-kissed schoolgirl. More beautiful still were the smooth and steady, purely graceful jolts she emanated.

"Beth! It's good to see you."

"I knew you'd be back." She smiled and tilted her head toward the subway. "Going down?"

Yes, it was definitely one of those days, Arnold thought, as he took Beth's hand and dove into the depths.

Margaret Yang and Harry R. Campion

Margaret Yang is the restaurant critic for the *Ann Arbor Observer*, and Harry R. Campion teaches English in Grosse Pointe, Michigan. They have been friends for nearly 20 years, and like to joke that they share a brain, since they finish each other's sentences even when not writing fiction together. They wrote "A Jolt to the System" shortly after they'd each moved to the suburbs, and found them as disturbing as Arnold Reale does in the story. They are currently at work on a series of near-future science fiction novels set in Detroit.

The Judges

J. S. Brady

My first encounter with science fiction was the weekly broadcast of *Star Trek* on NBC, back in '68 or '69. A few years later, I found an SF anthology under the living-room couch. I can't remember the name, but it scared me silly, and I didn't touch the stuff again until I was in Junior High. Then I fell in love with Andre Norton's *Breed to Come*, and soon was reading everything in SF/Fantasy that I could get my hands on, looking for what C.J. Cherryh calls "the good stuff." When I found it, it was better than anything, and usually even the less-than-good stuff was worth reading. I'd go without food in order to buy more books. Since then, I've become a professional writer and editor, as well as a professional computer geek. In a sense, it could be said I'm one of the people I was reading about as a kid. It's a good feeling.

Henry "Bud" Ensley

Born and raised in Toledo Ohio, I started to read about age 10, and it was SF. After a tour of duty in the Air Force, I now live in Minnesota with a wife, three cats, two hedgehogs, and sometimes a box turtle — who generally lives at the high school but comes to visit on holidays. I'm still reading SF. I have three book cases of SF and a whole public library just miles away with more SF.

Over the years I have expanded my reading. I even let my wife have a few mystery books on the shelves.

I have also learned that one of the places not to visit is any of the local book stores — costs way toooo much to visit.

Two of the series I like are "Harry Potter" — it is a great

grown-up type of book — and "Wheel of Time"; I'm waiting for the next book in each series.

Sometimes I have been known to go to work, just to get money for more books.

John Harnish

My involvement in various aspects of writing and publishing spans over four-decades—from letterpress to high-speed digital presses. My work has been self-published, traditionally published, and the three most recent books have been done with Print-On-Demand technology. My newest book, released in May of 2002 at the BEA, is *Everything You Always Wanted to Know About Print-On-Demand Publishing But Didn't Know Who to Ask*.

I am enjoying a life-long love affair with the entire creative process; I love a creative challenge. My magic smart paper from eons ago is in advertising design. As a Marketing Consultant at Infinity Publishing, I'm involved in start-up operations and new product introductions such as ATMs. I work closely with authors interested in gaining the many benefits available with POD publishing. I am a noted expert on the POD revolution that's gaining in popularity in the publishing industry.

Also, I am currently responsible for Infinity's annual writer's conferences and author's retreats, which I highly recommend.

Barbara Riley

I am a writer and editor living in Santa Fe, NM. I'm currently working on a feminist science-fiction trilogy, *Elements of Change*.

Anthony Ravenscroft

I am the guy responsible for the editing of the stories in this collection — as well as any lack thereof.

This is not done out of any meanness of spirit, or even editorial ineptitude. The stories in this collection (and the series) were judged upon their merits, including qualities of the typing process. Some of the entries would likely have advanced a notch or two if an editor's grubby hands had been applied. The editors have cleaned the text up a little for publication, but I expressly avoided messing with things too much lest readers be entirely in the dark.

There are no losers. Each finalist possessed some spark that appealed at least subliminally to our judges, managing to capture something of the human spirit growing to meet unexpected circumstances. I found a few of them personally touching, and feel that they sit nicely in the corpus of short-form fantasy fiction.

That's experience speaking. I've been a science fiction fanatic for more than three decades, anything from Verne to Stephenson, though I have a soft spot for Stanley Weinbaum and Walter Miller, and still light an occasional candle for James Tiptree, Jr. I'm proud to have encountered some stories they'd enjoy.

Susan Street

I have always been an avid reader, mostly murder mysteries. I was almost thirty when my second husband tossed me a book and said, "I don't care if you don't like science fiction, you'll like this. He talks about sex a lot." It was *Stranger in a Strange Land*. I read it and I was hooked.

As addictions go, the printed word doesn't ruin your health, just the health of your wallet. I read science fiction, fantasy, and mysteries. My guilty little secret is reading Oprah picks. I can't imagine who I would have become without all types of fiction to expand my mind and help forge my character.

To Purchase Additional Titles

You can order additional copies of this book or other products from Crossquarter Publishing Group.

Mail this order form and your payment to:

Crossquarter Publishing Group
PO Box 8756
Santa Fe, NM 87504-8756

Quantity	Product	Price (US$)
___	20 Herbs to Take Outdoors	$ 6.95
___	Attuning to the River of Kabbalah	$12.95
___	Beyond One's Own	$18.95
___	Concordance to The Book of the Law	$18.95
___	CrossTIME Science Fiction Anthology	$12.95
___	CrossTIME Science Fiction Anthology, Vol II	$12.95
___	Gods & Goddesses of the Zodiac	$ 6.95
___	Prometheus: the autobiography	$13.50
___	Shyla's Initiative	$12.95
___	Tellstones: Divination in the Welsh Tradition	$12.95
___	The Mercury Retrograde Book	$12.95
___	The Shamrock and The Feather	$28.95

Shipping ($1/item) _____

New Mexico addresses - add sales tax 6.7% _____

TOTAL _____

Name _____

Address _____

City _____ State _____ Zip _____

Phone Number (in case of questions) (___) _____

How are you paying (please check one):

__ Check made to *Crossquarter*   __ Credit card

Account Number _____Exp. Date _____

Signature _____

Please allow 4-6 weeks for delivery.